MERCY FLIGHTS

A Breakthrough Book no. 47

MERCY FLIGHTS
Stories by Mary Peterson

University of Missouri Press
Columbia, 1985

Copyright © 1985 by Mary Peterson
University of Missouri Press, Columbia, Missouri 65211
Printed and bound in the United States of America

Library of Congress Cataloging in Publication Data

Peterson, Mary.
    Mercy flights.

    (A Breakthrough book; no. 47)
    I. Title.   II. Series
PS3566.E7697M4   1985   813'.54   84−19490
ISBN 0−8262−0464−3

My thanks to the National Endowment for the Arts
for a grant that helped me to complete this book.

I would also like to thank the following for permission
to reprint stories that have appeared in their pages:
Ms., "Two Cats"; *Ploughshares*, "Traveling" (reprinted
in *Prize Stories 1979: The O. Henry Awards*) and "The
Carved Table"; *Fiction International*, "To Dance" (re-
printed in *Pushcart Prize III: Best of the Small Presses*);
North American Review, "With Evelyn" and "Coming
About" (the latter cited for distinction, *Best American
Short Stories 1977*); and *The Missouri Review*,
"Crows."

TO SUSAN WHEELER

CONTENTS

Two Cats, *1*

Traveling, *5*

To Dance, *17*

With Evelyn, *28*

Coming About, *36*

Crows, *49*

The Carved Table, *61*

Coastal, *64*

Like Boats, *75*

Mercy Flights, *82*

TWO CATS

He had sat alone a long time, nursing his scotch, watching Leslie Chase dance. It was pleasant to watch her. Her movements were lithe, sinuous, and her pale hair fell over her half-closed eyes when she bent her head. She was dancing with Riley but she was really dancing with herself. Perhaps she was dancing for him. Hadn't she, after all, told him that Riley was not important, was just a person she knew? It suited him, he thought, to be the one watching her.

Dressing for the party, he had chosen his best jacket and taken his favorite meerschaum pipe.

"You'll have good time," Mariko told him. She looked very small, vulnerable, and her eyes were so dark that in the light of their bedroom he couldn't see any depth in them. She looked, as he'd often thought, like a little girl. She put her arms around his waist, leaned her head against his ribs. The gesture warmed him.

"Won't you come along?"

"No," she said. "You go."

They spoke Japanese when they were alone together: for him, it was good practice, for her it was a comfort: they would go back to Japan one day. They had promised they would.

"I won't be late," he said. He lifted her hair; its heavy texture, as it always had, gratified him.

Now she would be alone in their house with their two cats: reading, or watching the television, or maybe mending his torn wool shirt. She never complained about being alone.

They had stopped asking why his wife didn't come to the parties. He had explained—so many times, so patiently— that she was Japanese and didn't feel comfortable with the language. That she didn't know how to dance and was afraid of being asked.

"Sounds like you're protecting her," they said, they all seemed to say. Every hostess came to that sooner or later.

"In a way, she needs protecting," he explained. "It's different, you know, to be native Japanese. There are matters of honor and decorum. Things a wife won't do, in Japan."

And, as he'd told Leslie Chase after one of the parties, things a wife will do. "She cannot ever know about another woman," he said. "About you. She would have to kill herself."

"Kill herself?" Leslie was half smiling, her fine mouth caught in a new expression that charmed him.

"That is very Japanese," he said. "A dishonored woman has no choice but to kill herself."

"That's medieval," she said.

And loyal, he thought. But this woman smells of flowers, she always does. "I'm American," he said finally.

He watched her dancing; she really didn't look at him. And the others dancing. Tonight's party was in Riley's apartment, and next week's would be elsewhere: but every weekend there was a party. The law students needed parties. The music was early disco and there were always enough drinks at the bar, and popcorn, pretzels, cheese and crackers that disappeared early. The wives tried to make fancy hors d'oeuvres. The air was thick with cigarette smoke and smelled faintly of marijuana. Each party seemed to have a different mood— tonight's was a kind of bitterness. They were nearing finals. He heard it in conversations around him; he spoke of it himself at the bar. They were all worn out, frustrated with trying so hard, and angry. This was a party with bad feeling. It would soon turn, he knew, to outrageousness—already the voices were louder, and some of the men were going more often to the bar. He too was tired, but not really bitter or angry; he had enjoyed a good week. He felt balanced, at ease. This week he had been favored by old Jones, Professor of Trial Procedure. This week he had declaimed in class and been praised for it. It was the reason people avoided him now, a little, or spoke perfunctorily and moved on. He was singled out as a success, perhaps even a star. Perhaps *the* star. He was different—older than the others, and he had worked for what he had, and he'd seen more of the world. They were rich kids. I'm not a rich kid, he thought, but I'm going to get there anyway. It was lonely, no question, but he'd come to believe you would be lonely. And lived with it. And thought, finally, it suited him. Just as his excellence on the tennis court suited him; just as his two lives, American and Japanese. In Japan, he had learned he could be happy. He had brought Mariko back with him from the army years; it was like bringing a part of the place that he could always own. Perhaps if his wife had been American, this business of ownership would have troubled him. But it was Japanese to believe you owned your wife. Part of being a man, of masculinity, to be at ease with such a role.

"You're not dancing," Leslie said. She sat next to him, her face flushed. He looked at the expensive gold earrings against the perfect neck, the slim arms, her thighs beneath the thin fabric.

"No," he said. "I'm not."

"You're a fair dancer," she said teasingly.

He saw they were alone in that part of the room, and he said, "I'm better at other things."

She smiled, and said something he couldn't hear.

"These parties are such a joke."

She touched his arm with her elegant hand. "I'm bored with dancing," she said.

When he drove home it was late, and he was a little tired, but happy, and the whole car smelled like flowers. The house was dark except for the small living room light Mariko had left on for him. Everything was immaculate; she had cleaned the kitchen, and on the couch the cushions were all in place, the magazines straightened on the table. Sometimes it seemed that no one lived in the house, but that it was all waiting. When the owners came back they would find everything ready.

He looked into the bedroom and saw she was asleep; he could hear her light breathing, and her hair was fanned loosely over the pillow. He pulled the door close, so the light wouldn't wake her. Then he used the bathroom, and went to the kitchen for a nightcap. She had left something for him on the counter.

It was a drawing, done very deftly in the Japanese manner, of two cats. One had its eyes half closed, and the other had its eyes opened. He hadn't known she could draw. She had written, "I am American," in English, in a small, careful hand, along the right side. It was like being inside a dream, to look at the drawing. But he did not want to make too much of it. Still, for a moment he felt unsteady, and he put his hand to the counter edge until it felt firm there again. A man cannot let the balance go out of his life, he thought, and he resolved that in the morning he would remind her of what she was.

TRAVELING

In April when she drove away he looked at his hands. They were oily from the boat's engine, from the garage. But what a thing to notice. He turned and saw the children, who were watching from the steps, and wondered what she had given him now.

The day before she left they discovered something wrong with the Volkswagen. He swore it was running on only three cylinders, but she refused to take it to the shop. "It runs," she said. "That's all."

"But it won't get you there."

"It will."

Yet, when she started it, the engine coughed and died. Warmed up, it raced too fast and he could hear her coming home a half mile down the road, sounding crazy, like a car without a muffler, a car with a problem. He didn't want her to leave that way. He wanted to trust the machine. That was the reason he did the premature tune-up and the oil change himself. And, too, it was the reason he urged a sleeping bag on her, in the trunk, although nights were warm. He wanted her to be safe.

When she had first brought up a trip alone he sensed she'd been thinking about it a long time and waited for the right moment. The time when she would tell, and not ask. In the last year he'd learned to expect statements from her rather than questions. Now she usually asserted what she would do. It was left for him to complain or to let it be. And usually he said nothing.

In the thirteen years of their marriage they had hardly argued. When they did it was startling and important, reminding him of the time in Rockport when they were first engaged. He was captain and she was crew in the interclub races. She knew what the boat was for him. Respected it, too. It put an edge on him to prepare for a race. The night before one, he never slept. Yet, even knowing, she had risen up in the boat like a witch or an apparition when he ordered her to tack. Had risen up and said, "You won't use that voice with me! Sail the damned thing yourself!"

They were heading out and surrounded with sailboats, and the whole harbor heard. The whole harbor watched.

"What do you mean?" he shouted. "Ready about!"

"The hell!" she screamed.

They had fallen upon each other in the cockpit right there, in the middle of the race, rolling and grappling like scrappy dogs while the boats sailed on past them. He was a mild man. He couldn't believe this had happened. She was all fire but he couldn't believe it happened.

Afterward he told her what she already knew: the town of Rockport wondered what he was doing with this girl.

But she loved him and she would marry him on the condition that they leave Rockport. It wasn't the race. Only that as long as he was bound by his family and the town, he could be no husband to her. Did he care that much?

When they married and left, people said he was making a great mistake.

If loving her was a mistake it was one he wanted to make. They moved to Maine where he worked as a county psychologist. The first years were hard and slow, and she was restless. But the children transformed her. She had an instinct for being a mother, responding to the world as half a child herself. He watched her feeling he was attending a great mystery.

And they didn't stop being lovers. She was small and alert; he was reed-tall and gentle. He made love to her carefully in the beginning, teaching her as he himself had been taught by a woman while he was still young. She was as ardent as he had been.

So they had grown together, but apart too. He sensed in her, always had, an urgency that the marriage did not address. Or a need. He told himself her childhood did it. She was her father's daughter, and the man had raised her to be wild and intense and loving and desperate. Her nature was like a continual accident. She seemed as surprised by herself as he was. But she told him she couldn't be other than she was.

When she first said she was going to Nova Scotia alone, he didn't know what to answer. Rushing ahead of him, she said how at nineteen she'd planned to go to Alaska with some college kids. Alaska seemed a great adventure. To go so far, she said, was like running out to the end of something and teetering, balancing, looking dead-on into mystery. Her mother had opposed the trip, but the arguments did no good. Finally she told her daughter she thought the group leaders were lesbians and it wouldn't be safe, traveling with them.

She had not gone.

But the idea rankled in her, oppressed her, all these years afterward. She said her instincts were to go; said that to argue it her mother had craftily run instinct backward into fear. And it worked. But left her feeling fundamentally failed. Something, she said, was stolen from her then. She couldn't name it. She wanted it back.

"It's because I have to do it," she said, turning that familiar look on him, her eyes so utterly blue they reminded him of the hearts of glaciers.

"Yes," he said. Just the word.

Leaning over the fireplace she talked until he better understood, or thought he did. When she went down the long driveway, the Volkswagen engine racing and exploding, one arm out the window waving goodbye, he understood less.

*   *   *

"I'm getting to know the kids better," he said when she phoned on the third night.

"Daddy plays ball with us," Paul said. "And he's good, Mom."

"He makes hamburgers better than McDonald's," Elisabeth said, pride in her voice.

"We miss you," he said, taking the phone again. He held it balanced against his ear, looked at the kitchen mess, cat food smeared on the floor.

"I miss you too, darling."

She said she was staying at a wonderful hotel directly on the ocean, and she would probably spend the remaining time there. Said she was fighting the impulse to go antiquing. That she had found a painter who did wonderful risky things with color and shape, and if his smaller pieces weren't too costly she'd bring one home. "Imagine a royal blue sky!" she told him. "The color of Elisabeth's jumper! Can you see it?"

During the day he went to work and the clinic felt the same as it had. His patients—but he preferred to call them clients—were unchanged by the change in his immediate life, and he listened to them closely, sorted their confessions and fears as if he were scrying a very precious object. But what he wanted to read in them was the form of his own life.

At night when he came home the children were there and waiting. He announced that meals would be community business and they would all take a hand at cooking. Elisabeth made a banana cake with food-color blue frosting. Paul made hot dogs, carried them proudly into the dining room. Some nights they all cleaned up together. Other times, dishes

from two days stood in the sink. It was not that unusual—
she didn't do dishes faithfully either. When she cleaned, it
was always with a violent activity that left nothing motion-
less: chairs, books, lamps, his mother's bone china. Elisabeth
and Paul instructed him in their mother's routines and he
tried to follow them, or adapt them for himself.

And he saw how generous his children were. Wondered
what part of it was his own doing, what part hers. In their
conversations over dinner he asked them questions that they
answered more honestly than he would have thought possible. They were original, these children. At nine and ten
they had an essential goodness about them. And they were
fair. Old enough that perhaps they would carry these quali-
ties into adulthood. He felt a pride that was embarrassing,
even uncomfortable.

She sent postcards in the mail: "Dear Everybody. I love
you and miss you all. The weather is perfect. When I eat
alone I think of you hard. That's the worst time."

He never doubted, even for a single moment, that he
wanted her to return to him.

*　　*　　*

When she was back, she did not seem much changed. For
a few days she talked eagerly about things she'd seen, the
thrill and fear of being alone in a strange place. But matters
of the children, of the house, pressed them both into familiar
patterns. Before long he expected dinner at night again,
drinks before it. Paul and Elisabeth stopped asking him to
play softball with them.

He felt a warmth with the children that wasn't there before, as if they shared a secret. But he reminded himself that
the secret was only their privacy and the small things they'd
learned while she was gone.

They discovered they were lovers still, as if they had

doubted it. He learned again the good security of being in bed with her. The third night she was home, when they lay in the dark looking at the window, he searched for a way to tell her. She was warm against him.

"There was a man in Nova Scotia," her voice came from the silence.

He waited, listening.

"He bought me dinner, and a drink. Took out all the pictures of his wife and kids. Even one of the family Doberman, for Christ's sake." She sat up and turned to face him in the dark, intent, like a Buddha. He couldn't see her face.

"I thought, what does he care about me?" Then she laughed girlishly. "Then I knew why it was."

His question was in his silence.

"I told him I was tired." She leaned forward and he imagined her face, what it had. What did a face hold? Only more information, to help along a conclusion. Still the reality was that when they were apart, they were separate beings.

"He wanted another drink," she said. "I was flattered. He wanted me to stay with him."

He cleared his throat, thick from so much silence. "You're an attractive woman . . ."

"Middle-aged," she said. "They don't treat you that way anymore, at my age."

He realized he hadn't expected this, or feared it either. "I'll never know what happened, really," he said, as much to himself as to her.

"But nothing," she said too soon. "Really, just nothing."

*   *   *

It seemed to him they didn't spend enough time together. When he came home from work and they sat with gin and tonics, their conversation was good, encouraging, but not . . . he wasn't sure. Only that when she described her talks with Barbara, with Amy, they sounded more interesting.

There was an energy that he seemed to miss, keep missing. As though she had things for these women she didn't have for him.

It came down to the boat, finally. Last summer they had bought a twenty-six-foot sloop with savings—it was that or work on the house. Now, their second summer, he was eager for them to be a family on the boat. The children were no problem. Elisabeth was a good sailor, a natural. Paul, though he was often sick on board, refused to leave even during the worst times.

It was different with her. She loved the boat, she said, but not as he did. Said she would cruise with the family but not just go out and sail in the harbor as he liked to do. That was dull. She had other things. He didn't need her company always. Couldn't he understand?

No, he could not understand. Beyond that, she should know. She'd seen him fool with the engine all winter. Seen him drive to the marina when the boat was hauled out, just to look at it.

She said she understood he needed to unwind. He needed these weekends. But she needed her time too, and when he took the children to the boat she had her chance for privacy, for quiet. They were good enough words, and he thought he believed them. Their force carried him all the way to the harbor. Yet when he rowed out and climbed on board, prepared to get underway, he felt only that she belonged there with him.

So he argued. First he said he missed her. Then, when she wouldn't hear this, he said the other men with boats wondered about them. Other wives sailed. "People will think something's off in our marriage," he said. He was unable to keep the accusation from his voice.

"People will think!" she exploded. "Damn them, let them think what they want!"

"What do you have that's so important?" he asked her.

Her look was like the one before she'd announced her trip alone. As though if he didn't understand, he should not ask. As if asking was the worst insult.

But he wanted to know.

If they were a family, if she was his partner, he reasoned, then they should be together on the boat. She had her days alone.

But those were for children and housework, she said. It was the other time, private time, that she needed. She reminded him that the boat made her seasick.

He reminded her that she behaved like a perfect fool on board, eating sardines and corn chips and drinking beer; taking Dramamine that only made her dizzy. "It's in your head," he said. "Psychosomatic."

The arguments silenced her to a point where she went grudgingly to the boat sometimes, whole-heartedly others. Still, she accused him of an internal logic that tangled himself with the boat, her love of him with sailing. It wasn't so. She could separate these things, and God knew she wanted to. Couldn't he see she needed time for herself, after the pressures of family, of the town?

He caught himself wondering if there was another man. Stopped himself from wondering it.

*   *   *

In August they had planned a whole weekend on board, and she refused to go.

"This can't be," she said, pacing the length of the front windows. She stopped and looked out at the pine woods. "I'm lying to myself. To you. Sometimes I like sailing, but not so often as you. You can't force me to."

He looked at her standing there, her arms folded.

"The boat's become an issue," she said.

"Anything would be."

"But this is the one for us."

"I don't understand," he said.

She said she didn't expect understanding, only tolerance. She wouldn't be pressured any more—"bullied," she called it. She accused him of failure of imagination. How could he want her on board, when she hated it?

"You won't give it a chance," he said.

"Damn it, what have I been doing all summer?"

When she left, he sat in his brown leather chair, and the house—his own house—felt like a stranger's. He was as uncomfortable there as an intruder. He reasoned with himself that their problem was an inability to live with differences. She was right, he couldn't understand her distaste for sailing. But he was right too, in wanting to share what he loved most, with her.

He found her in bed, lying face down. It hurt him to see her bent, tense shoulders. He felt the loneliness and distance coiled in himself around the hollow it was making, had made. He didn't like feeling this way. "I'm going to the boat," he said.

She murmured something into the pillow.

He crossed the room and got his jacket, came back and sat on the edge of the bed to change his shoes. "I'll spend the night there."

"All right," came her voice from the pillow.

"It's not an argument," he said.

"I know."

"Just . . . something."

She didn't sit up. He stood, and with the jacket over his arm, bent and kissed her hair. He wanted to say more, but he was afraid of the words. They might become something he didn't mean.

It was a clear night, and the air was soft. He drove with the window rolled all the way down, feeling the air on his face. The moon was almost full and there were thin clouds around it. On the River Bridge he could see the harbor lights, and the stars as well. There was smoke coming from the factory.

What do I feel? he wondered, checking himself for feeling.

Down Kittery Point Road toward the harbor, he drove slowly looking at the houses with their lights and their dark lawns.

There were no other cars in the rental lot. As he walked along the dock with the oars on his shoulder, he listened to the bell buoy ringing out in the harbor. Water slapped on the dinghies and bumped them against one another. Their boat was moored quite far out, but he could see its beamy shape from where he stood.

The water was calm, and in the quiet, feeling the tug of the oars against the tide, he felt himself almost to be a trespasser. Still, the secret feeling was a good one. Even in the dark, this was a world he knew.

Their boat rocked in the night like a seed pod, moonlight on her decks. When he crawled on board and tied up the dinghy, he felt something hard and tense let go inside him. The boat was an island and he was safe on it. He knew everything, here. If anyone came, he would hear the creak and groan of the oars in the locks. Even she would have to come that way.

As he unlocked the cabin, pulling the boards from its opening, he thought how privacy was what he'd wanted. He wondered if she understood that. Not to get away from her or from the children either. Just to go to what he knew. The boat was the best place. He had done all the work of painting and repairing himself. The damned winches had had to be ordered from England since the boat was English in design—made for the Channel—and he'd done that too. He smiled. He had done all of that.

He sat and lit a cigarette, wondering what she thought now. Imagining her, he found in himself a smugness that was surprising. He had been thinking: now you will understand how it felt, to stand on the lawn and watch you drive off to Nova Scotia. To leave us. He had been thinking it all the way to the harbor, his arm out the window. That she was getting hers, now.

That was detestable. It said things he didn't want. Said how much he was hurt by her traveling without him. More than that, how resentful. But the worst thing it said was that he wanted to punish her. He hadn't known that, didn't want to know it now.

He felt the boat rocking. Usually the harbor sounds relaxed him. All the noises of water, metal, and wood. And over his shoulder, the rotating beam of the Coast Guard lighthouse. He liked all of it. But like wasn't enough. Loved it, by God. It was home to him. And she didn't love it.

The resentment was gone, not because he'd wished it but because it was worn away. That was a small part anyhow, not substantially true of his feeling for her.

He wondered what *was* true, then. The emptiness he had felt when he looked at her lying on the bed? Yes. The hollowness? That too. Not only true, but growing in the last year. She was changing. More of her was secret to him than had ever been. Her fire had always been a mystery, but a wonderful one. And now there was this . . .

So a man had to wonder what to do. He thought of the children. In the last year he'd loved them not less but more.

He tossed the cigarette into the water. It made a curve of red light, then was gone.

Do I want a woman? he asked himself. But he knew the answer. They were different, he and she, but he loved her. Perhaps even more for the way she pointed up their differences.

He thought that maybe for him it was this night alone on

the boat, just as for her it was that time in Nova Scotia. Well, if that was so, she had courage then. He had to admire her courage. What else could it be, to risk him and the children, to drive off alone such as no woman her age ever did, certainly nobody in town? The risks of middle age were less dramatic, but then the stakes were higher. He was alone, now. Still, he thought, in going to what we love, we don't deny anything. When he looked, the boat had shifted in the tide so the point of the main mast seemed about to pierce the moon.

TO DANCE

The woman who can't dance moves in with the Arthur Murray Studios dance instructor. When he learns of her affliction he misunderstands her motives in wanting to live with him. She reminds him that they met quite by accident at the counter in Grant's and that she was drinking a root beer and minding her own business. He addressed her first, wanting a light for his cigarette. This alone would not have been enough, except that half an hour later while he was having his picture taken in the little booth with the gray floral curtain over the door, she poked her head in thinking it was empty.

"Neither meeting," she reminds him, "had anything at all to do with dancing."

He is reassured and, convinced that love can conquer, resolves to teach her to dance.

"You won't believe this," she tells him, "but it is absolutely impossible to teach me to dance. I have never been able to dance. Never, never."

"Can you tap your fingers to a record?" he asks her.

"Not if I'm listening to the words of the song."

"You can walk, can't you?"

"I didn't walk until I was seven years old."

"You can run."

"Well," she says, "that came later."

"The human body operates according to rhythms," he says. "We learn to carry a beat while we are still curled under our mother's heart."

"I think," she says, "that I learned the sound of my mother's spaghetti dinner and it had no rhythm at all."

*   *   *

"When did you discover the problem?" he asks kindly. She notices the way he strokes his chin, like a doctor. They are lying in bed and he has the other hand on her thigh.

She tells him she was in college and they were required to take a physical education course. She had never wanted to learn to fence, and tumbling seemed somehow immature. Then, she says, she was invited to the Senior Gala. But she tells him that when she was small it took three years to learn the moves for hopscotch. "How far back do you want me to go?" she asks.

"I don't want the story of your life," he says.

"No?"

"I want to create you myself."

"I've been trying to do it for years," she says. "It can get very dull."

"But you never danced in high school?"

"My religion forbade it," she says, so well he believes her.

*   *   *

"It seemed to me," he says by way of explanation, "it was time I moved in with somebody. I'm twenty-two years old and I've never lived with a woman before. That can get to you, you know?"

She stands in the doorway to the bathroom watching him shave. The bathroom mirror is steamy from his shower and the one window is made of gritty frosted glass. The shower curtain has lily pads and goldfish on it. He bought it at a second-hand store, he said, because it was "campy."

"I'm older than you," she says.

"I know." He turns and grins; she begins to wonder what
he wants. "But don't tell me how much. I like there to be
mystery between people."

"My college major was philosophy," she says.

He splashes water against his face and reddened neck.
"What?" he says, reaching for the towel.

*   *   *

That evening he brings home some records from the dance
studio and says she will have her first lesson. He opens a
paper packet in which there are many yellow gummed feet
marked R and L. Kneeling, he places them on the floor in a
pattern.

"L is for Left, and R is for Right."

She has been watching and has already figured this out.

"The waltz is perhaps the easiest dance to learn," he says.
"We usually start there and work up to more difficult ones.
You'll get the idea."

"I doubt that," she says.

The stereo is playing a very elementary waltz. Listening,
he begins to count. "ONE-two-three, ONE-two-three. You
got it? ONE-two-three." He snaps his fingers on the ONE.

She remarks that he looks very much like Lawrence Welk.

"Beat the time with me," he orders. "Think of your
mother's heart."

One-two, she beats with her hand against her thigh. But
delays before the three.

"You're putting me on."

"I tell you," she says, her eyes filling up, "that I can't keep a
beat. My mother was a smoker and her heart was irregular."

He opens his arms and asks her to come stand on his feet.

They go around the room this way for a while, and he
marks a deliberate, caricatured beat with his feet while her
own feet slide off his and find themselves tangled between his

ankles. She spends most of the time trying to get her feet on top of his again.

When the waltz finishes they are both exhausted.

*   *   *

The next day when she wakes at noon he has already left for the studio, and she finds the little yellow feet glued carefully to the floor in the diagram of the waltz. The record jacket sits ostentatiously against the stereo. The apartment is very quiet. She holds her breath until she thinks she is having an anxiety attack.

She goes into the kitchen and puts coffee on the stove. From the kitchen she can see all the way past the stereo into the bedroom, where her two baby-blue suitcases lean against the door. His telephone is in the bedroom. She thinks of making a phone call, but how can a woman tell her mother she wants to come home from a man with whom she has lived for only two days, who is trying to teach her to dance? That taxes, she thinks, the natural endurance of any mother.

The yellow feet show clearly on the living room floor against the stained walnut boards.

*   *   *

Later she sits on the couch with a book. She suspects he will be home soon. The book is one chosen from his shelf, a cheap edition of a spy thriller. Such a book, she reasons, should hold one's interest from the very first page, become gripping within the first chapter, entangle one in speculation and intrigue by the middle, and rivet one to the couch for the startling and improbable climax. She finds that the book does none of the above. The main character is soggy and badly drawn. The plot is elementary. Nobody loves anybody. The murder on page seven is not credible. The drawing on the dust jacket does not enhance one's image of the action.

Closing the book, she thinks about her life. She, too, has not had a lover for a long time. Too long. However, she did once live with a man. It lasted several months. He worked as a busboy, and later she found out he was playing the numbers. When it ended she decided she would not do that again with any seriousness, since one could be damaged. Then she thinks this reasoning is just equivocation. The real reason is that she is chronically unable to see life except as a series of ironies, and in this context one decision seems as good as another.

Take this young man, for example. For a dance instructor, he is not very attractive. Oily, she would call him. She realizes she might have bought a parakeet as easily as moved in with him. The choices that day were absolute—large and small options. Anything was possible. Now there is the problem of deciding whether moving in with him constitutes a large option.

One doesn't move in with a man one hardly knows.

Or one does.

She realizes that her view of life has been amoral for a long time and that she is surprised by nothing.

*   *   *

"Didn't you ever watch American Bandstand?" he asks her over their Hamburger Helper. "Didn't you do the calypso and the lindy with your friends while the TV was on?"

"No."

"I dated a girl who was a Girl Scout once," he says, "and she told me how they'd have club meetings and spend the whole time dancing with American Bandstand. It was in Philadelphia, you know?" He closes his mouth over the hamburger.

"I was a Brownie," she says.

"Maybe the waltz is too hard," he says. Inspired, he picks

up the plastic knife from beside his plate. He asks her to
hold the knife in her right hand, and he runs to the living
room to put the record on. "Beat time!" he says when he
comes back. "Against the table!"

The classic strains of the waltz reach from the living room
into the kitchen. She closes her eyes and imagines a ballroom
in Vienna. Then she sees the studio. He is bending and glid-
ing over the polished floors with the lovely girls who enroll
with Arthur Murray. At a distance he looks very sophisti-
cated. Never mind the cha-cha, she thinks—the rhumba, the
calypso, the samba. Never mind the mad erotic dances of the
steamy equatorial regions. This is just the waltz. The good
old waltz. Simple beat, nothing to it, it will do. *And I can do
it.* She raises the knife and brings it down on beat two.

"ONE," she says loudly.

"That was two."

"I'm sorry," she says, opening her eyes.

"Don't be sorry, for God's sake. Try it again! ONE-two-
three, ONE-two-three."

"What's the name of this waltz?" she asks him.

"'The Blue Danube.'"

"Don't you have something more modern?" She glances
into the living room. The lights are out—except for the
occult blue of the tuner—and she can't see the yellow feet
any more.

*   *   *

The next afternoon he stands in the living room wearing
bullfighter-tight pants with scarlet and gold spangles down
the sides and a silky black shirt with full sleeves. He clicks
his heels together and snaps his fingers. "Today," he pro-
claims, "we learn the rhumba!"

"Oh God," she says.

"I mean at the studio. Want to come watch?"

"Please," she says. "Don't." And retires to the bathroom.

*   *   *

She realizes she wants to give him a gift but is absolutely without a sense of what might please him. Finally she goes to a record store and buys a recording of the minuet. When she returns home this album looks absurdly out of place in his collection, and she puts it at the back of the stack where he may never find it.

"How did the dance start?" she asks him that evening.

"Which dance?" He is getting a carton of chocolate milk from the refrigerator.

"All dances."

"How should I know?" he says. "I'm only an instructor with Arthur Murray."

*   *   *

She tries to identify how she feels in his apartment. A guest? A friend? His lover?

"I passed through his life like a kidney stone," she says aloud, making words to formulate the experience. She wishes they were more funny than they are.

She goes into the bathroom and stands before the mirror, leans over his shave cream, his acne pads, his brush and comb, his squeezed tube of toothpaste. Reminds herself that they have certain things in common. For one thing, they both live in the same city. For another, they were both at the counter in Grant's on a Saturday morning. That says something, she reminds herself.

*   *   *

That evening over hot dogs they have a lengthy discussion about talent, in which he tells her of all the minor talents he has never yet explored. Photography. Calligraphy. Block printing. Pastels. The recorder. Poetry. And he has always wanted to learn serious acrobatics.

"You must have some too," he says encouragingly. "Aren't there disciplines you've always wanted to take up?"

"No," she says.

"What do you do with your free time?"

"I masturbate."

"Don't be cute," he says.

*   *   *

"I'm off to the studio!" he says the next afternoon. He wears a black tuxedo with smooth satin lapels. In his buttonhole there is a little plastic white carnation. He spins and dips to his knees, stands again. "Voila!" he says.

"Marvy," she says. She is standing in the bedroom door, still wearing her bathrobe. She notices that the yellow feet have been removed from the floor. Some floor wax has come off with them and there are dry, ghostly marks of feet dancing the waltz.

"I may be late tonight," he says calmly. "Don't bother with fixing dinner."

After he has left, she finds herself immersed in major problems of ethics and free will. She paces through the rooms. Stops to look at the uninteresting black and white prints he has framed and hung in uninteresting ways on the white walls. She notices the imbalance between the geometric black and white curtains and the very obvious decorator fake-fur yellow pillows on the white corduroy couch. Somebody sometime must have told him these arrangements were artistic. The plant in the window is an air fern because these require no care. It is too green. Probably, she thinks, they dye air ferns.

Something, she thinks, has been missing in my education

to be an adult person capable of reasoned choice. Some urgency. A vision of her mother and father comes to her, the photograph of them before the old frame house on Birch Street. They look like an *American Gothic*. Except that her father holds a garden hose and her mother wears a Villager blouse with small tea roses on it. They seem wrong to her. Not stalwart enough. Lacking Christian and Patriotic fiber. A life that should have been easy and filled with guidelines for right behavior has instead been given to her full of inconsistency and chance and improbable turnings. The old values were better, she thinks. Now we don't know anything. She wishes her friend had a recording of John Philip Sousa.

Meanwhile, her friend is at work in the Studio she has never seen, retracing with his slim young body all the traditional gestures of movement. It seems to her he has unconsciously fitted himself to a system of values that she has always lacked, always wished for. To dance, she thinks, is to return to the old forms. They were something to count on.

She pulls the bathrobe tighter around her waist and looks out the plate glass window at the brick wall of the next apartment building. All this intellectualization becomes finally a waste of time, she thinks. Turning one's wheels. The reality is that here I am in the city in his apartment, and the window is dirty.

Choice comes to us unbidden. We know which way to go. In his dresser drawer she finds an extra set of the yellow feet and takes them into the living room. She goes to the stereo and puts on the recording of the waltz. Carefully she sorts the feet, putting all the Right ones into a separate stack. When she kneels to the floor she folds her bathrobe back from around her legs.

Her skin is white from no sun. She frowns at her legs, at the loosening flesh of her thighs. Already middle age is setting in, middle age and its complexities. Somewhere along the pike, she thinks, I should have gained more ease in living than I have. At thirty-three, she thinks, I don't even know how to pass the cheese.

Not that he notices. His needs are relatively simple. He makes love like a man performing a function, a man reading on the toilet. She would not believe him to be a dance instructor. But he told her he learned to walk on tip-toe. "How nimble," she said, thinking of the nursery rhyme.

Kneeling, she peels the brown backing from the Left paper feet and arranges them one by one in a deliberate fashion going straight toward the door. In the bedroom she can see her opened suitcases. The waltz blares against the apartment walls; the waltz climbs the striped paper on the window wall and clumps itself up under the ceiling, pulsing.

"It's important to find the beat," he said. And she asked, "Why?" He told her to think of riding the subway. If you don't have the rhythm of commuting, the air doors will close before you've entered. But she argued that the crowd moved her faultlessly into the train and the doors closed neatly on everybody; she argued that it was easy when you were pushed by a mob. "You only think so," he said. "Think again."

She thinks of rhythm. Lies back and wonders whether she will follow the feet out the door. Wonders whether she loves him. Love should be easy; it should be instinctual; it should make its own new patterns each time. It has never been this way for her. The garage mechanic was enthusiastic but mentally dull—he made noises that sounded rehearsed. The accountant looked at his watch. The insurance broker wouldn't stop talking. The whole world seems to be a nightmare of indifference, of missed connections.

She raises her legs and observes how the flesh loosens down against her hips. When her legs are raised they are almost lovely—slim calves, after all, and good firm ankles.

The thighs are a problem, but when they make love he doesn't notice.

The waltz blares through the room; it sidles along the varnished floor and clasps itself around her shoulders. Her bathrobe slips sideways. She extends her white arm. Runs a hand down her leg and pinches the skin—like a chastising parent, like an eager lover. Vienna and the Grand Ballroom enter her from the top, find their way to her hands. Her tiara glistens, spins points of light. She speaks softly to her partner: Oh, a marvelous time, of course I am beautiful. Her nipples are Renaissance spires. ONE-two-three, she forgets him. The sun is on her legs. Her fingers believe they could waltz along forever.

WITH EVELYN

Evelyn, lose weight! I'm thinking. But, because she is not *my* ten-year-old daughter, I don't say it and only keep combing her wet brown hair all of a piece down her glistening back, while she faces the mirror and stands still as a mushroom, expressionless. My big breasts keep brushing her shoulders and she doesn't notice, or doesn't acknowledge them anyhow. They are probably uninteresting to her, my childless breasts, oversized, sometimes an embarrassment to me and sometimes the amplest of offerings, but I am not overweight at all; I've only these cow-breasts that swing down under the baggy sweatshirt, cotton rubbing my nipples. *Anything more than a handful*, the boys used to say, *is too much*. And laughed. And pointed. But *Evelyn! You have handfuls around your young waist, blanketing over your hips, and more handfuls bunching over your thighs, and your shoulders are round with fat and your upper arms jiggle so: at ten years old!* And maybe the boys are talking. I don't want you to think *that* should matter, dear Evelyn. Not boys. Not yet. Anyway. What matters is your fat passivity, your uncommitted eyes, the way you always say, "Yes, please," and "no, thank you," as if you were visiting strangers every weekend. *These things count, Evelyn.* Though you don't listen, and pull your towel tighter.

I hear rain starting on the skylight. It's only nine A.M., but already I've made breakfast eggs and tidied up downstairs and seen that the water was right for Evelyn's shower, sent Andrew (her father) off with Dennis (her brother) to bring in more wood for the stove, set the whole works going.

28

They looked at me with a devilish mixture of resentment and relief, and went. "Evelyn," I said, "you're going to get cleaned up."

"Yes, thank you," she said.

I grab the spray bottle of No More Tangles and give her hair a squirt. Then I go at it with the big plastic comb, jerking away. Her head snaps back, regains posture. Her expression doesn't change.

"Does this hurt, Evelyn?"

"No. It's fine."

Am I a sadist? I try to be more gentle, start the tangles from the bottom and work my way up slowly, unraveling the problem hair by hair. She seems to smile. Perhaps now I am doing it right, now I am behaving properly. Or it is only the ghost of a smile in the foggy bathroom mirror, just a distortion, breath on the glass. As for me, the tension starts in the soles of my feet (where it usually does) and works up the calves; then my legs are rigid. I try to stop it there, flexing my knees, bouncing up and down a little, and my breasts swing under the sweatshirt. She doesn't ask me what I'm doing. It happens every time she visits anyway, and she must be used to it by now—the shower, the complaints of dandruff, the thick hair all stuck together oily and neglected, the bouncing stepmother. If I had a daughter of my own, she would have big breasts and thin, easy hair. She would take showers without being asked. And she would learn to comb her hair alone at an early age, to be self-reliant. I would teach her, among her first words, the lines from the 1855 *Canadian Settlers' Guide*: "In cases of emergency, it is folly to fold one's hands and sit down to bewail in abject terror. It is better to be up and doing." Not because we are Canadian, which we aren't. Because these words are good life advice.

Evelyn's hair is a case of emergency, this very minute. It combs down smoothly now and has many lengths—two or three inches longer in some places than in others.

"Did your mother cut your hair last?"

I have uttered the taboo word: *mother*. There is an important silence. Then she says in a grave voice, "Yes."

I sigh. "Well, she must have been in a little hurry when she did it."

"Maybe."

"Because it's all different lengths, Evelyn."

Silence. The potent silence of meditation. The bathroom resonates.

"I guess," she says finally.

I take a deep breath. "She must have been in a *great* hurry, dear, and I would like to do something. I want to use my scissors to even out your hair. Evelyn, I would like to trim it. I will not cut it shorter, but only straighten it out. What do you think of that?"

"All right," she says flatly.

"I want to ask you a favor, then," I say, pressing on. "Don't mention this to your mother. She may not like it." *This is an awful risk*, I think. *I'm asking for complicity*. Is *that* what I want? I comb the hair down and wait for a signal from Evelyn. What was it she said about her mother, yesterday? That Mother was staying home this weekend to watch the neighbor's dogs. *Guilt*, I thought. She *guilts* this child. And then I realized I don't even know what Evelyn's mother feeds the children, much less if she watches dogs. That I'm doing more than taking risks: I'm violating. This little girl will choke on it. The tension has reached my lower back now, and it aches. *Now Evelyn should say No! I'm thinking. No! I want my hair the way Mummy cut it.*

She inclines her head to look at me from behind a curtain of wet hair. I can't read a thing in her expression. "Okay," says Evelyn.

Scissors in hand, I begin to cut. *Evelyn! I'm thinking. I'm about to cut your lovely thick hair all the way up to your*

*eyeballs, and you will never look the same way again. How
do you like that?*

The evil stepmother raises the gleaming shears for an ordinary chop. The little girl is silent and patient, gazing into the
foggy mirror.

*　　*　　*

Last night I woke at four A.M. worrying about this child. I
put my hand on Andrew's damp sleeping back and looked at
the shaggy, dark pines through the window. He was snoring
gently. His sleep begins with violent noises early and fades to
pianissimo as dawn approaches. Six years married, I could
tell the time of night by his sounds. We have found Evelyn a
friend here in town, and Judy was over to play earlier last
evening. They had a game called "Trouble" with dice that
roll by popping a plastic dome in the board's center, and
they reached and popped the dome and moved their little
red and yellow markers around, and never said a word to
each other. They didn't laugh, or giggle, or tell secrets. They
popped their bubble with a gravity scarcely equaled, and it
seemed that if I took the game away they would still be leaning into neutral space for something to touch. So I went into
the guest room to play the piano. After a half hour, when I
was rendering "From This Moment On" with teary senti-
mentality, Evelyn came in and sat on the couch. *The music
has reached her*, I thought. I realized that I hadn't heard the
popping plastic for a good ten minutes. I revved up. I ended
the piece with a great flourish of chords, hit the final note
with a fine attack, and turned to her smiling.

"Judy and I are bored," she said. "Is there something to
do?"

We went into the living room, and dug out another game.
I got them started playing it. I did not go back to the piano.
I went into the kitchen instead and made a fresh pot of coffee

and wondered when Andrew would come back with Dennis—they had gone to the market for a few things and must have run into somebody. Andrew cannot go out without taking an hour or longer to talk. To anybody. Marketing is, for Andrew, a social occasion. Now Evelyn and Judy played "Uno" with vengeance, slapping cards on the table. It was the only sound in the house and I turned on the radio, which was rather like inviting additional guests to a dull party.
Judy is a gorgeous child with red hair, and I've seen her with other friends: they're noisy and silly and vivacious and energetic. Once when I entered her living room, Judy and a friend were doing headstands on the rug. Once they were having a salamander race. The problem—if there was a problem, and there *seemed* to be one—was not with Judy. Judy was growing breasts now; they poked forth under her t-shirt like spring crocuses. *Perhaps Judy is outgrowing Evelyn*, I wondered.

I lay in the dark that night listening to Andrew's breathing and wondered. I pondered Evelyn's silences. Her sluggishness. The way she came in for lunch with her brother, and sat on the couch in her jacket and hat until after ten minutes I said, "For God's sake, Evelyn, aren't you hot in all those clothes?"

"I guess," she said, and went to take them off.

Four in the morning is The Hour of the Wolf. More people die just before dawn than at any other time of day. There was no humor in my thinking, no relief. I was stark awake looking at the ceiling, then the west window. *The child*, I was thinking, *is a menace. And she is worrying me. And she is not even my child*. And then—because these were true things, and I felt them all the way to my stomach—and because it was four A.M. and I was without daytime defenses—my eyes filled up with tears that ran over and down my temples into my hair, and I just lay there that way, hating and loving Evelyn, until I had to reach for the box of Klee-

nex on the bedside table and blow my nose, and Andrew
stirred and rolled over to wrap around me, one hand over
my spilling breast.

It did not stop the crying. I was thinking then of the other
thing Evelyn does, which is reach for Andrew. Wherever he
is, she finds him, she touches him. On the couch she rubs his
shoulders or his feet, she puts her head in his lap. When we
returned Judy to her parents, Evelyn ran along the sidewalk
behind Andrew until she'd caught up to put her hand on his
back. She went in the door that way; he seemed not to notice.

He never talks of the children when they aren't with us.
For him, the children are a long memory of screaming and
worry, baby bottles and diapers to change, cat food on the
counter and dinner unprepared. But on these visitation
weekends, he is capable of turning around and picking
Evelyn up and hugging her so fiercely she winces with pleasure. All ninety-six pounds of her. When he does this, his
son, Dennis, pretends to be fascinated by a book or by the
birds at the feeder. And I watch and remind myself that she
is his daughter. After all.

*   *   *

I hear the door open downstairs now; they are coming
with armfuls of damp wood. The rain is only starting. Cold
rain, the weather report says, for two days. In two days,
Andrew will take the children back to their mother.

I would like to deliver Evelyn with a note attached, I think
now, finishing the trimming of her hair. I pick up the hair
dryer and turn it on high, and because it is noisy and pro-
hibitive of conversation we both relax. I lift Evelyn's hair
from beneath and feel it falling in wet pieces over my hand.
The note, affixed to Evelyn's coat lapel, would say, *Dear
Joanne: Your daughter needs more love. Sincerely, Karen.*
Andrew and I have a united opinion about Joanne: we can't

stand her. But privately I wonder how it must be to raise kids alone, what she must be thinking when she cuts her daughter's hair with a chain saw, who she consults when the bad grades come back from school. Maybe her daughter has enough love.

When I lift my arms over Evelyn's head, I look into the mirror and think, *I should have had children*. At least one child—the breasts seemed to demand it; the heart beating under them wanted it more. I would not have to give my own child back. And sometimes—the best times—she could curl in my lap, and I could bend my head and inhale the sweet warmth of her hair, and she would put one hand against me and fall asleep. I'd have the scent and touch of mothering, as well as events, squalling, disagreements. My child would want to know who I was. But stepmothering is like trying to set up housekeeping on an ice floe: every motion abrades. Evelyn and Dennis never ask where I came from. I married their father when Evelyn was four, and probably it seems to her I have always been around, like the painting in the living room, the pewter pitcher, the brass candlesticks. I am a feature of their lives, but problematic: not friend, not aunt, not mother. They don't know that I had a dog named Trivet, nor that I was a fat child, nor about my own abusive mother who—although she is dead—visits here with me at the oddest times. And they don't know that Andrew and I had a two years' war, and he won: no more children. He has practical notions about children, my Andrew. They cost money; they demand time.

So I stand in my tatty sweatshirt and jeans in this steamy bathroom, lifting fat Evelyn's thick, wonderful hair, and it separates like strands of yarn before they are put on a loom, texture without pattern or weave, unfinished. She is the closest thing I have to a daughter, this child with her mother's eyes. The rain comes down harder, and downstairs I can hear Andrew and Dennis laughing.

"Why are they laughing?" Evelyn says.

"What?" I turn off the hair dryer, pick up the comb and attack again.

"Why are they *laugh*ing?"

"Oh, probably they like what they're doing."

"Like us," says fat Evelyn, smiling into the foggy mirror.

Her round cheeks pull up, and her eyes crinkle. In spite of her weight, she has a pretty smile. I find a bad snarl and bury the comb there. *More than a handful is too much, Evelyn*, I think, working away. *It breaks my heart.*

COMING ABOUT

Sido carried the cold paper sack of six-packs low before her like a pregnancy. When she reached the dock she stopped, foolish with the brown bag in her arms, its damp bottom edges pressing to her thighs. She wore shorts, a navy t-shirt, and a white sailing hat she had bought too small and wore for spite at herself because of that carelessness.

They were loading things onto David's lobster boat—two chests of ice and plastic sacks of meat sandwiches, fishing rods, bait in paper cartons, and the jackets and sweaters. None of them saw her. She hated unfamiliar situations—when she didn't know the rules—and being on the dock was one, and she wished uselessly that David would know and come help, but he did not know, and there was nothing to be done. She hiked up the bag and wished for height behind it, for stature, but she was small. Then she wished for a miracle of sudden knowledge about boats and going to sea. All wishes failing, she went down the steep ramp, and they saw her, and Steven waved.

It would not be a good day out. Fog still drifted into the harbor from the gray North Atlantic, although it was eleven. He had hoped the fog would burn off. She didn't know fog, though now it looked worse than when she'd left to go to the house for the beer he'd forgotten.

He was on board, checking the boat. Sido thought he looked oddly severe, like a military officer.

"It's his wife," Steven said behind her.

She nodded without turning.

"Leslie just left."

"Why?" she asked, watching David. She couldn't imagine anyone leaving him. He climbed to the bow of the white boat like a cat, supple and quick footed. What an interesting, cold man, she thought. What a remote man. She considered that she might or might not wish to know him better. But she did know him.

"Something with the kids," Steven said shortly. He took the beer from her arms and handed it across to the woman wearing a bandana scarf who stood on the deck of a small sloop tied up between the dock and David's boat. Then he cupped his hands to his face. "We should get underway before noon, dear," he called to David. The accent was thick Down East: *deauh*.

When she turned away, Jess was coming down the dock toward her. He was David's close friend and the only one who really talked to her. She knew she warmed to strangers slowly; she was bad at cocktail parties; when people didn't interest her she forgot them. Then later she regretted herself. She had hoped to be new and vivacious with David, but she always found herself not new. She also knew that she wanted him to love her and that Jess saw and suspected her for it. Well, she thought, I'm suspect, and I'm guilty. It was a matter of accepting. She reminded herself that she was thirty-two and divorced, no kid.

Jess put his arm around her shoulders and said, "Hello, Love," into her ear, bending to put the words under the brim of her hat. She stiffened. She looked into his muddy green eyes and then let her eyes fall as far as his barrel chest. He wore shorts and a denim jacket and a look on his face of huge disdain for everything. He was golden and large. She wondered suddenly what the flesh of his chest would feel like; but it would be under her fists.

"There he is," Jess said in a smug voice. "Admiral David.

See him?"

"Leslie was here."

"Oh, she comes by, now and then." He grinned, white lines disappearing around his eyes, and he moved his legs just apart and set his shoulders. But he was graceful.

"Is he really getting divorced?"

"Sido." He touched her arm. "I think he really is."

"What does she want, coming down here?"

His answer was David's of the night before: "She doesn't know what she wants."

"Neither do I," she said, although he wouldn't believe it. She squinted and turned away.

"I do." He slid back and opened his arms. "Enough money, sex, good food. I know just what I want."

"But you're a hedonist, Jess," she said, on cue.

He smiled. Well, that's finished, she thought. That little exchange, that time. And she was suddenly exhausted. She turned to see the boat, where David was stowing things below. I'll probably go out and be sick all over the damned thing, she thought. That would be like me. And David will take care of it. And Jess will see, she thought, watching the fog come in.

*   *   *

His beer can was carefully snug up against the window and he stood with both feet braced wide apart, a cigarette tight in his lips. He watched the sea. The fog was dense and impossible, and her own eyes burned from peering into it. She looked too hard, and now she saw shapes where there were none: a ridge of ghostly trees that looked like shoreline, a schooner rising up from the swells, birds flying near the water. But her eyes were lying. The sea was empty, and whatever lay beyond the fog was out of their vision.

"You ought to sound the horn, Davey," Steven said. He sat on the edge of the gunwale, his fishing hat with its long brim pulled close over the light hair that curled up under it. His thick mouth curved open, showing white teeth.

David pressed the horn and it went like a voice into the fog. There was no answer. The boat drilled strong and hard into the rolling water.

Sido had been sitting near Steven, getting used to the motion, and now she stood and tried to walk forward. She had to grip the rail, and she paused and lurched again while they watched her. David raised his empty beer can and asked her to pass it to Steven. He motioned for another.

"When your mother was an alcoholic you don't drink beer," she had told him. "You don't get a taste for it because you still see her lying on the couch all blurry, embarrassing you." He had nodded, but did he know what she meant? He had put his arms around her then and kissed her neck, did he really know what she meant?

Stumbling over the gear box, she got his beer and brought it back. He lifted it. She stood near his shoulder watching the water.

"Too bad it's not clear," he said. She raised up on her toes and saw the bow rise and dip again with the waves. "I wanted a good day, but I like fog too." He half turned and put his arm around her waist. "You're so quiet," he said.

She stood planted near him in the boat that was a perfect mystery to her and felt the rolling ocean that was vast and strange in the fog. She felt the desolation of their course, a boat loaded with fishermen. She said, tipping her face up to him, "I'm having a good time!"

"Want to run it?" he asked her, and moved from the wheel.

In his place, she put her feet as his had been and felt the boat give under her while he explained over the noise of the engine how to use the wheel to bring it back on course within two degrees. He said they were going eight knots and their course was to Boon Island. He said you could not ever be exactly on course but you could keep it close. She nodded,

watching the compass needle slide over: When she had the
feel of the motion, he turned and went below, leaving her.

The wheel balanced against her hands. It moved, she drew
it back. The water hissed against the bow. She let the wheel
give to port and come back again, holding it with a lift in
her right hand. Anticipate it, he had said. Feel it coming. It
came to her that she had never wanted to learn anything
quite so much as she wished to learn this boat. She didn't
care about being a fool, a beginner. Her back was to them.
She wanted the muscles in her legs and shoulders, in her
arms, the pull of the wheel against her hands, the tossing of
the boat, all to gather up and be one thing. Standing firmly,
her legs taking the shock of motion, she made her hands go
lighter on the moving wheel. When he came back she realized she had forgotten him.

*   *   *

David took the boat to a fishing shoal where the depth
was sixty feet, the four men got out their rods and bait,
and David cut the engine to let her drift. Sido and Gail, the
woman in the scarf, sat watching and eating sandwiches. She
couldn't remember Gail's husband's name: the last was Run-
lett, but the first had gone by her. It was too late to ask.

Jess took clam necks from a carton and held them up.
"Sido!" he called, dangling the clams. "Aren't these something?" They hung like miniature penises.

"All you think of is sex, Jess."

Jess laughed, as if he knew her too well. He threaded the
slippery clams onto his hook.

She shook her head.

The fog had lifted but there was a silvery haze along the
shoreline, and silver too on the backs of the waves. She stood
and went forward, intending to crawl up on the bow. She
had her sea legs now and didn't care that they watched her.
When she went past the cabin she took a flotation cushion

and slung it over her shoulder like a pocketbook. David watched her. He was tired; she saw it in his face. She wondered how many of the men knew they had had only four hours of sleep the night before, and wouldn't they be amused by that, and wouldn't they tease him? If they were alone on the boat they would be urinating over the side rails, making jokes about David being worn out, for he might tell them about last night. She wondered, would he tell them?

"Don't you want to fish, Sido?" he called.

"No. I'm going up to lie down."

"You can go below."

"I'd rather be in the sun."

She crawled forward and lay on the white-painted bow. It rolled now and again as if to toss her. Finally she moved the cushion to a spot below the cabin and lay on one side with the cabin against her back. They drifted about three miles offshore. If the men caught fish it would be an afternoon of fishing, she saw now, and if not it would be an afternoon of moving from one spot to another looking for the fish. Jess had caught a dogfish but no one, yet, had a haddock. They wanted haddock or even cod. They had said they wanted bluefish but no one was too hopeful. Blues weren't running yet on the Maine coast. She couldn't imagine the fish on the bottom of the sea, even imagine a depth of seventy feet, although she had fished in Midwestern lakes when she was small. Her father had been a good sportsman and had loved the water, and he probably would have loved the ocean if he had ever seen it. He had been like David, preoccupied, a man who knew guns and hunting dogs and fishing. How strange it was to be with such a man. She had spent the last few years, and all the years of her marriage, with university people. David was not an intellectual. He was a practical, organized man who loved his family and who had not wanted a divorce. But Leslie was a little crazy. Now he said of it, "It's happening. I don't think about it much. It's just happening."

As if it was a weather system. And she knew Jess accused
him of rebounding with her. She knew Jess warned him
against her. All of which seemed to imply she wanted him,
wanted to land him just as they wished today to take the
fish, but it wasn't true. She had met him in the resort bar
after a day on the beach. They had got drunk and danced
together. One thing led to another, though she'd sworn to
herself since the divorce she would not attach herself to a
man again. Well, she thought, lying on the rocking white
bow, do I love him or not? Perhaps it is only summer, just
the kind of poignant thing that will happen in a summer, as
in a war. When winter comes, even autumn, it will be over.
She did not know how she would feel when it was over. There
would be an ache in her for the boat, she knew now, but
would there be an ache for David? It came to her that she
might love two things—him, in a way she was not yet able to
define, and the boat too, the good balanced feeling of the
boat. Perhaps it was this: that with David she did not feel
balanced and at the helm of the boat she did. Perhaps the
two things worked together to make one. But she wondered,
if it was truly one thing, then what was the future?

Her sense told her that summer clarified. Summer made a
whole all brilliant and warm and of itself, and when it ended
the thing ended. You could look back on a summer and see
it entirely and not expect anything else from it. To haul a
summer feeling up into the next season was difficult; it
didn't ride well. They were living a resort life now, she almost living with him, and it had its own implied ending.

And hadn't she promised herself never to fight the
endings?

"Sido!" he called from the helm. "Move back. We're getting underway."

She rose up on one elbow. "No. I want to stay here."

"You're sure?"

"Yes."

"Then hold on."

As David started the engine, Jess came up the side of the cabin to sit with her. They felt the bow raise as he opened the throttle, and Jess watched her. Damn it, she thought, I've been around boats before. I know enough to hold on, for Christ's sake. She frowned at him but he was looking away. "You treat me like a child," she said to his profile.

"Just being careful."

"I suppose you think I don't know the sea is lethal." The waves were silver and cool and the boat rode the swells, and she watched them break from it, churning white water.

"Touchy women bother me," Jess said.

"I'm not touchy."

"Defensive, then," he said.

"Now we're coming about," she said, feeling the boat turn.

"No," Jess said. "That's for sailboats."

She wanted to ask him what about his own marriage, defunct last year, and to tell him he was not perfect as he wished to be and she could see the little scars, like scratches on a gold ring, all over him. He had been imposing and suave since he was in prep school, since puberty—he was that kind of man. The only thing the years had added was a patina; he was better worn, he gained luster that way. It wasn't hard to imagine him at fifty, still big chested, elegant. He was so much a type of man she caught herself up, fearing she imagined him.

It was not like this with David. David was real. He worried and he forgot the beer, and he wondered what would happen to his children after the divorce, and he was kind and when he put his arms around her he spoke her name over and called her Sweetheart, and he fell asleep faster than any man she had ever known, positively dropping into it.

When he was asleep she lay beside him thinking, going slowly, then having alpha visions. He would not understand even if she could explain to him, and she was sad for it. She had found the sleeping almost at once as their place of departure. She would not have chosen that place, given a choice.

Yet it was for this stability that she valued him. She could deal with her own hallucinations: she would fear his. She had learned to live with the pain of seeking after herself: she could not bear it in him. Yet he didn't know her, she knew he didn't know her. And Jess, sitting so near her, believed surely that he knew her, but he was wrong.

Jess pointed off to starboard, where a brilliant jellyfish floated just under the surface, its dull, lax streamers of tentacle drifting away from its gorgeous cap.

"I've never seen one before," she exclaimed.

"Never?"

"This is only my second time at sea." She pulled her hat down to shield off the sun and looked out over the billowing water.

*   *   *

When they had stopped a second time she went back to the stern. Steven baited a hook for her and she sat on the gear box and cast a line into the water with the men's. Gail was not fishing. She watched the sliver of line run down into the water, her thumb on the reel. When it had touched bottom, she locked it and drew it up again four turns. The clams would float there. David came to sit near her and put his arm around her shoulders, pulling her toward him. It was a geature her husband had made; before she had time to think, it warmed her.

The men talked about the fishing and when they thought the blues might begin striking, and Jess—who had also come back to fish—explained you got blues, like striped bass, by trolling, not by dropping a line, but it was only more information and she only half heard it. There would be no fishing, and no boats either, after this summer, unless she was able to find a way herself to have one. She sat with the refracted sunlight on her shoulders calculating how long she would have to work, and with what income, to get a boat of her own. Then she drifted with the idea: a sailboat or a lobster boat? And how big? What to name it? And where to put the mooring?

There were so blessed many things in the world that she wanted, and the list still grew. It wasn't money, she didn't care for money, but she did care for the things money got you. Since she'd gone to graduate school she had been broke all the time, and she was weary with the student life, hand to mouth. Money got you travel and dance lessons and clothes that were a pleasure to wear and the silver bracelet you wanted in the League of Craftsmen's Store. It got you Oriental rugs for the living room and a house that looked out to sea. It got you the horse you'd wanted since you were eight years old. You could buy time for yourself with money. You could find interesting people, because you would be where they were. Then she shuddered. It was vile to think so much about money. She had been safe and happy without David and she would be safe and happy without him again. She would remember the summer and what he had taught her about boats; she'd be damned if she longed for it. Everything in her life now, her own life in New Hampshire, was chosen and precious to her—the boots she had bought with the first paycheck from the temporary job in Boston last year, the plaid wool blanket, the tools for her car, books she liked, clothes she found on sale in the good stores. In spite of student poverty she had done well enough; it wasn't a league for boats; it wasn't a league for summer houses on the Maine coast; there were things missing in it. But there were people she loved, and she had a direction.

Jess had said to her, "He hasn't much money, you know. It's in his family, but he hasn't much himself."

And she was angry, too angry to speak. As if she had been thinking that way of David or counting on anything from David. As if she would have stayed with him for any reason other than his gentleness with her, his sense. The rest, the trappings of wealth, was a holiday. You don't hold on to holidays, though if you're lucky you find them, and if you're calm you enjoy them.

"What do you want?" David had asked. They were lying on the couch together. He had reached for his scotch and water and she had rubbed the bottoms of his stockinged feet. She was drinking orange juice with ice in it. It was midnight. They had spent the day together. They had talked about her family back in the Midwest, and about how she did not see the ocean first until she was twenty, and about her love of the water. It had been easy until he asked her what she wanted and then she was stunned silent by the question, answers chasing one another around in her mind, all of them equally lies, all of them equally honest. She would have said, When I'm with you it's you that I want, and when I'm away and alone with myself I'm not sure. Then she would have said, I want you because I created you before I ever knew you, even, at eighteen, imagining a love affair with a man named David. She might have told him, I want you because you have brown eyes, and I do, and you write left handed, as I do, and you call a cat "kits-kits-kits" just as I do. But her mind turned instead to what she had known and wanted before she met him, before the boat and the silver water, before she had tried to be close to a man again. I want to be whole, she would have said then. I want to be myself all entire. I want

to work and value it. I want not to be afraid of what I can't
be, or what I can't do. I want to let go.

She looked at him and said, "I want my work to go well."

He nodded.

"I want to live near the ocean."

"Yes," he said.

"And I think I want to be close to another person, some
day, although that's been unimaginable to me for a long
while."

"Your divorce."

"Yes."

"You were hurt?"

"Everybody gets hurt in a divorce," she said. "I had the
most god-awful civilized divorce in the world and everybody
got hurt." She wanted the thing she said to ring down into
the real depths of him. She wanted it to sound there where it
was not so easy any more to love anyone. She realized she
had wanted to tell him the truth.

*　　*　　*

Late in the afternoon, they had only five fish. The sea
churned in the boat's wake and David gave her the course to
steer toward Kittery Harbor. They would come straight upon
a red buoy first, he said, and then swing the boat around and
in. He said there would be currents and she should watch for
them, since they would lift the boat and pull it about. She
nodded, squinting into the light. The sun was low in the sky,
but they had plenty of time before it went down.

David went to sit with Steven and Gail, and she heard
them joking. She wondered what the rest would say of her
when she was off the boat. How they judged her, David's
new woman. It was important to him what people thought.
His wife was making a mess of his life right now, phoning
everybody, embarrassing him, and her drinking made him

worry for the children. Sometimes when she had been at his apartment, Leslie had phoned and put the children on the line to say goodnight to Daddy—he called it "playing mind-games with kids"—and when he hung up the phone and came back she could see the cords standing out in his neck.

She spotted the red buoy and glanced back at him; he pointed the direction for her. Now they were in the mouth of the channel and the swells had changed to a quick chop that made the front of the boat jerk. She felt it in the wheel. She felt it under her hands. She had to move quickly to re-cover course. Listening back, she heard David talking with Jess now.

In a minute he would take the wheel from her, since she could not dock the boat alone. She would give it to him and become a passenger again, David's special guest, and she might go back to sit with Jess and watch while David brought the boat into the harbor as easily as if he had trained it with his hands. She didn't know if he would ask her to go again. Perhaps she would not be on this boat again. But she would give him the wheel; it belonged to him. She would go astern and take out a bottle of ginger ale and sit with Jess, and try to talk with Gail, wondering how the day had been for them. She had hardly got to know them.

She was glad the fog had burned off, giving them a silver ocean, and glad she had gone to the bow alone. When he brought the boat up to dock, whether or not he loved her, she knew how she would leave it and she knew the solid feeling the dock would have under her feet, how she would say goodbye to them all and thank them, and David, and then she knew what she would think later. That it would have been nothing. It would have been easy.

CROWS

For weeks, it seemed—since her thirtieth birthday—the crows had been noisy around the house. Karen watched them through the kitchen windows after Michael left for the office. They liked to fly from the tall, dead elm on the harbor side, to the other elm, as bare and dead, toward the back two acres and the small field. Often she counted as many as seven, large and glossy. She looked at them through the binoculars. They were supposedly among the most intelligent of birds. She thought they were ominous, and she didn't like them. They were loud, and they startled her when she walked the retriever—one even cawing from a branch only a few feet over her head, insolent.

Michael, who had lived in the country all his life, thought her attitude was funny. One night he jumped at her from behind when she was doing dishes. He made a funny *caw* sound, and gripped her shoulders.

"Stop it!" she said, stiffening. "You're being horrible."

"They're only birds."

When the dishes were through, she told him she didn't like to be teased, or surprised. She said she wasn't used to the country and the crows made her uncomfortable. He was sitting across the room in his favorite chair—he had a boyish shock of dark hair over his eyes, and whenever she became serious he affected an abused look that only annoyed her. Now he was pouting like a child. He refused to listen. Well, she would *make* him listen. How did he think it was for her to be so lonely in the country or with his friends who never talked about anything but snowshoeing or hunting? Their wives, even the ones who had jobs, talked only about recipes and new drapes. And she had to shop in the stupid little town where he worked. And she had to try to get along with his children. She wanted—he should know—more: dinners out, movies, friends who knew about the world.

He rubbed his chin and asked her with moody eyes why she had married him, then.

She sat at the table, facing him. She had thought about it a lot, she said, and she'd decided he was a different person when they were going out. After all, they had met at a bar in *Cambridge*. He had taken her to restaurants. Once, when she mentioned a book she liked, he'd said, "If you care about it so much, I'll have to read it myself. I want to know everything about you." And he had read the book. Did he remember? Did he know how much he'd changed? Just last week he'd tossed away the newspaper article she left out for him. Now, since they were married, every day followed the same routine. They had stopped going out on weekends. She told him they were becoming boring, dull, like old people. "I can see us at sixty," she said, "staring out the windows with our morning coffee."

"Is that so bad?" He had given her, he reminded, the first house she had ever had.

In the morning, when he'd left for work, Karen put out mixed seed for the sparrows, the towhee, the cardinal. She filled the tube feeder with thistle for the finches and the window feeder with sunflower seed for the chickadees. The chickadees were always the first to come in, the least timid. Sometimes they nearly collided, and then they made a silvery musical noise like coins sliding into a purse. She watched him while she had her second cup of coffee. She moved her chair closer to the window, to see if they'd trust her. Perhaps, she thought, one day they'll eat from my hand. Michael said they didn't need to feed birds in summer, but she did it anyway.

It was their first summer in the house. Fog drifted in almost daily from the ocean and made the wood countertops swell and distort. The cupboard doors wouldn't close. Towels mildewed unless she washed them often and left them in the drier a very long time. She had time to do that. And that was the trouble, she decided now: too much time.

When she was twenty-six, and had worked in Minneapolis for seven years, she went for a walk along the Mississippi River one important Sunday afternoon. There, she assessed her skills—typing, dictation, office management, bookkeeping—and found them adequate, her work history so respectable that she had not taken a day's sick leave in three years. She had an apartment with tall ceilings in a brownstone off Lake Street. There were places in the city she especially liked: a coffee house on the West Bank across from the university, a specialty store on Hennepin Avenue, Lund's Market where she bought groceries and good cuts of meat. It was better than Braham, the small town of three thousand where she'd grown up.

Along the river, she had remembered the magazines in her apartment that showed pictures of glamorous Eastern cities, cities with history, and the excitement that informed the glossy, posed photographs. She imagined herself there. She was tall, although not beautiful. There was a kind of grace in her movement, and she wore clothes well. She had long, thick hair. She imagined herself bending to look into a shop window on Beacon Street, her hair falling against her face. She realized that she was restless in Minneapolis, and bored. When she considered, again, the Mississippi River, she knew that she wanted more.

Six months later she had a job and an apartment in Boston. In the morning she rode the subway from Kenmore

Square to the financial district where she worked. The side-
walks were red brick, and from her office window she could
see the Customs House clock, and, almost, Boston Harbor.
This was a very long way from Minneapolis, and farther still
from her home town where she had impatiently ridden her
bicycle along the curved sidewalk toward the Baptist church,
and where she'd attended high school events and sat on
chipped wooden bleachers. This was a new life.

In Boston, she was an administrative secretary, and she
bought a small imported car and handsome clothes. Often
she visited a *pâtisserie* off Boston Common, where she drank
thick French coffee and read the *New York Times*. She had
worked in Boston just under two years, and had a few friends
there, and sometimes went out on dates, when one day in
the *pâtisserie* she looked up from her newspaper and saw
that the floor was dingy, and her coffee mug was cracked,
and in the corner there was a man making faces at nobody.
Her life, she realized, was not exciting at all. Her job had
become routine. She was rather shocked, and she felt somehow cheated.

Only a few weeks later, she met Michael at a bar in Cambridge. He told her he didn't like the city, but since his
divorce it was more interesting than sitting around at home.
He drove down from New Hampshire to see her every weekend after that, and they went dancing. He was a heavy
drinker, but she didn't mind—the more he drank, the fun-
nier he was. And he was thoughtful; he gave her little pres-
ents, a neckchain, a scarf pin with an amethyst. He had a
wonderful New Hampshire accent, and he told her long,
drawling, Yankee jokes. She imagined that, with him, she
might find everything that was missing from her life.

After they were married, Karen gave herself six months to
get the house in order, and then she would look for a new
job. Women dream of houses, she told herself. It sounded

old, like old music, a fugue. Women plan them, imagine them, furnish them in their minds. Just as they imagine the husband, handsome as Michael was, coming home in the evenings. Waiting for him, she felt she was waiting for more than Michael: as if he might come home changed. She disliked herself for being unhappy. She watched him drive up while she peeled carrots at the sink, dirty curls of orange. She thought, I'm lucky. But lucky was a kid's word, a rabbit's foot, a horseshoe, a four-leaf clover. It was like telling herself how to feel. "You're late," she said when he came in. "You don't come home early like you used to." He had stopped to have a beer with his friends; they had planned to go fishing.

"The crows chased away my birds again," she said, thinking, How dull are the daily stories of women. She was embarrassed for herself. She thought quickly, Have I done *nothing* all day?

His ex-wife lived only a half-hour away; there were two children. When Karen and Michael looked for a house, they planned a room for the boys. It was off the living room, and Karen called it The Guest Room when the boys were not visiting, and The Kids' Room when they were. She was their stepmother, but she hated the word. In Snow White, the wicked stepmother, the queen, is forced to dance to her death wearing red-hot iron shoes (in the Walt Disney version she is pursued by dwarfs and leaps into a bottomless chasm). So much for stepmothers, Karen thought. She asked the boys to call her Karen, and tried to think of herself as their aunt, or as a remote friend.

The boys were formal when they visited. They even asked for a glass of water, like little guests on good behavior. Their mother said when they came home from visiting their father, they fought like animals for two days. The boys had eyes like Michael's, but the feral, pointed faces of their mother. In profile, especially, Karen found it hard to look at them. She showed them the crows, and they counted the birds together on the dead elm one weekend. Five or seven or eight—they kept shifting. The boys were not impressed. What are crows compared to lasers or to robots that talk? Karen told them how she'd watched the crows chase a hawk across the property, over the field, flying so low near the car she could have reached up and touched them. She tried to make the information interesting.

*   *   *

That Saturday night, after Michael had taken the boys home, they talked over dinner about the winter's supply of wood that would be delivered soon. They talked about projects to complete around the house, and Karen got up from the table to add them to the list fastened to the refrigerator door. Michael said nothing about the children.

"Do the boys like pulling brush with you?" she asked finally.

"No kid likes working."

"We might plan activities for them. Movies, or fishing."

"There isn't time for fishing. I'm not an entertainment committee for kids anyhow."

He salted his food, coating it with a white layer that made her nauseous, and she turned her head away. She picked up her wine glass and looked out the window, where it was growing dark. She looked at the shapes of tree branches; they seemed almost oriental, like a brush drawing. Pink light spread along the western horizon—it touched the water in the harbor with luminous, faint color.

"When you're working again," he said, "you won't have time to plan fun and games for kids."

"But don't you love them?"

"Sure, but it doesn't do a whole lot of good. Now, does it?"

She held her wine glass and felt something she couldn't understand; a disappointment, near to sadness. She wanted to imagine closeness with his children, with Michael himself. Perhaps, she cautioned herself, it's a dream happiness: laughing boys and happy fathers, a greeting card, an old, optimistic movie. Still, couldn't it be like that if something changed?

Michael paid no attention that she wasn't eating. He took a forkful of potato and said he wanted to hunt the young retriever for the first time this fall. She was green, he said, but with a little work she might come along.

"If you shoot one of the crows," Karen said suddenly, "they'll probably all leave. That would be practice for the dog."

She surprised herself, saying it. She had always disliked guns, even her father's guns. Michael had a rifle, a .22, and a pistol, all stored in The Guest Room closet, but they were not loaded and not dangerous at all. Once when the boys visited, he had given them target practice with the .22, and she hadn't liked that either. Yet she imagined him shooting a crow and felt quite suddenly elated. *That* was the thing to do.

"I can't use the rifle," he said. "The firing pin's off."

"Use the .22."

"You can't shoot a bird with a .22."

"You're a good shot," she said.

The next morning after breakfast, standing at the kitchen window in her yellow bathrobe, looking at the light fog, Karen reminded him of shooting a crow. The idea seemed to make him nervous. He paced, lit up his pipe. She told him it would be only one crow, a warning to the others. And that when the crows were gone, the songbirds could come back, the cardinal, and even owls. She watched his face change, look younger and more intent. She watched his eyes. She saw him decide. She turned coolly away. Something was loosened in her, another self—one that wanted to pursue, to hunt, to connect. And to kill? Perhaps. Or perhaps she only wanted a definite resolution. It was a new feeling, a strange one.

She dressed, and they went out. Michael still complained. He said there wouldn't be any crows, but Karen was certain there would be. They went down the gravel driveway and then crossed to the small opening into the grassy field at the back of the property. Michael carried the gun. The retriever trotted along with them, eager. Karen listened; she looked into the woods. There was, of course, a crow.

"In that tree," she said, pointing.

The crow was near the end of an oak branch, halfway up. It was low and close and didn't move except to turn its head toward them. Karen stepped back. Michael braced his feet and raised the gun to his shoulder. He made—it seemed to her—a perfect line from shoulder to wrist, all one thing. For a moment, she felt a chill fear of him.

The gun made an abrupt crack, and the dog jumped sideways and turned pantingly to look at them.

"Did you see that?" Michael's voice was higher. "Did you see him move?"

She looked up. The crow was still on the branch.

"I hit him," Michael said. "He almost lost his balance."

Karen saw that indeed the bird's wings were spread slightly, and it wavered.

"Watch," Michael whispered, and motioned to the dog. The dog was excited, but didn't know where to look.

"Now she can retrieve her first bird," Karen said.

They waited. The crow didn't move. Karen had never heard such silence. Finally, after long minutes, it lifted spread wings. "He's bleeding," Michael said.

Karen watched the crow lift from the branch, lift and fly, very slowly, away toward the harbor. She saw the streak of fresh blood on the bird's glossy breast. She couldn't believe it flew.

"I got him just under the neck," Michael said, "and the damn thing's flying."

"But won't he die?"

"Sure, maybe in days. The bullet went right through."

It wasn't enough. *It was not enough.* Karen felt anger flashing all through her, like summer lightning; like lightning behind dark blue clouds, too far off for sound.

"We have to try the elm," she said, breathless.

"I've already shot a crow."

"The others won't know," she said. "He's gone."

"This is no way to kill a bird."

But she was walking already, toward the front of the property from which they could see the harbor and houses opposite.

There were two crows in the dead elm.

"I can't shoot toward houses," Michael said. "A .22 bullet goes more than a mile."

"Then get down beside the tree," she said. "And shoot toward the mud flats."

He looked at her. She felt suddenly as she had when she was sixteen. She was with her boyfriend in his big Ford Galaxy driving through her home town. They passed the school superintendent's house, a man she hated. "Gun it!" she said. Before he thought, the boy floored the accelerator, laying a strip of rubber fifteen feet long on the residential street. They were picked up by the police two blocks later. The boy, who had a previous offense, lost his license. Karen lost nothing. Nor did she regret. It was a moment of control, of pure power.

Michael went through the tangled brush toward the harbor, the same brush he and the boys had been clearing out, to get a better angle on the crows. She stayed near the house,

keeping the dog with her, watching him. Michael went
slowly, until he found the right spot. Then he raised the gun.
She saw the line of the gun against his shoulder. The shot
exploded.

One crow flew up, and the other staggered. Clung.

"Again!" she shouted.

He shot again, and the crow jerked sideways a second
time. But held on. The other came back, circling, calling.
Fly. It returned to trouble, beating its wide, dark wings,
wanting the other to escape. The wounded crow held.

"That's all, damn it," she heard Michael say.

     *   *   *

From the house, they studied the wounded crow with
the binoculars. It was hunched down, head sunk into shoulders, and its beak was open. Michael thought he saw blood
coming from the bird's mouth. Still its feet held on. They
agreed that the crow was probably shot in the neck and that
it simply couldn't last that way.

But late in the afternoon the bird still clung, still held its
head at that odd angle, beak open, as if stopped in place. She
and Michael did ordinary things. She tidied up around the
house; he cleaned the shop. She remade the beds in The
Guest Room. They had dinner late, as they usually did on
Sundays, and it was too dark to see whether the crow had
fallen. They watched television. She watched Michael. He
had been right, of course; you can't shoot a bird with a .22;
crows are tough creatures; a .22 bullet will only go through
the bird, and if you don't hit a vital organ it can live for a
long time.

In the morning there were three crows, like sentries, in the
dead elm. The wounded one was gone from its spot.

Michael went to the office, saying he was sure the crow
was dead on the ground. Karen was not sure. That morning

she took a long time with her bath, a long time dressing in jeans and a flannel shirt. She looked at her hands. They did not seem right to her. They were shaky, and they seemed older. Michael, she thought, was a good hunter. Her father, too, had been a hunter. If he hadn't died, he would have taught her to shoot. Then she herself would have held the gun and tried to kill the crow. She might have failed to hit it. Perhaps, she might not even have tried. It was a matter of responsibility. But this thought did not reckon with the excitement she still remembered.

When Michael came home for lunch that noon, she asked him to go down and look for the crow. "I'm wearing a suit," he said. "I'm not dressed for it." She demanded that he go. Finally, he went grudgingly. Karen followed him to the edge of the lawn, thinking of what she'd done—not able to name it. Of what she continued to do.

He came back and said, "The crow's still alive."

"No."

"It's on the ground. I pushed it with my foot. Still alive, and shot through the neck and through both eyes."

"Blind?" she said.

They went inside together, and Michael went into The Guest Room. When he came out, he had the .22 in one hand and was putting bullets in his jacket pocket with the other. His face was impassive. "Let me tell you something about crows," he said. "There's no point shooting them because they just come back. You learn to live with them. I got those birds yesterday because of you, and I'll put this one away. But I don't want to hear any more."

Karen watched him through the window and wondered if she had made a mistake, marrying him. But the mistake would have to work backward, she thought. If Michael was wrong, then perhaps Boston was wrong too, and Minneapolis, and thinking this way made the choices of her life fall away against each other, reel backward, and she was dizzy, as if somewhere there was a first choice that might have been more right, or true.

But choice, she realized, was also immediate: it was in the room with her. She stood beside the blue chair and watched Michael walk off with the gun—this was a choice. For she had always waited, hadn't she? There was something ugly lying in the brush under the trees, dark, and suffering. *Boston will do it.* And she hated that it suffered. *And later, Michael will.* The crow was sacrificial, and she knew that she was the cause.

She did not want to think that all night long the crow had clung to the branch, that sometime before dawn, or before they were up, the bird had fallen. That it lived. That the other crows knew it. She turned away from the window when Michael went into the bittersweet carrying the gun. But she did not prevent herself from hearing the one necessary shot that finished it.

THE CARVED TABLE

It was her second marriage and Nan sat at the round table in Marblehead with her new family listening to their conversation and thinking of what her first husband would see, if he were there. He would notice, she thought, my new mother-in-law's enormous diamond, and he would see this new father-in-law's yachting jacket, and he would be disgusted. Might even say, "What are you doing here? You'll lose your soul to these people."

There were six around the table: she and her handsome husband, his parents, and her husband's spoiled-looking older brother and his glossy wife who tossed her fine red hair and laughed at the right times, and made little asides to the mother-in-law while the men held forth. Nan envied that sharing. She envied her thoroughbred sister-in-law who did not take it all so seriously. Nan took it too cruelly seriously, and she couldn't shake off the feeling that something was terribly wrong.

She touched the carved wooden edge of the table with one hand and with the other, she reached toward her husband and rested her hand on his knee. He was always quiet during the cocktail hour, but also he listened with an odd, fixed smile: one of complicity, mesmerized, like a twelve year old trying to learn the hard lessons of being an adult. When you were an adult you drank a lot; you kept up with your father in the drinking. This was difficult, since his father went to the bar for more bourbon often, and with each new drink he grew louder, and with each he had more to say and less that

made sense. The man was well educated, she reminded herself, and certainly he knew much about banking, airplanes,
and stocks. Yet he believed that children on welfare should
be allowed to die, so we could purify the society. He believed
in capital punishment. Believed we should step up the arms
race and show more muscle abroad. Wars are different now,
she wanted to say. We have nuclear weapons. We should
have a different set of rules. She did not say these things.
Neither did she say that his capitalism created in the minds
of the poor a need: they saw the television advertising, they
saw the consumption of goods. How could they have any
dreams but the ones he himself had? No wonder, she wanted
to say, that the Cadillac sits outside the tenement and at the
market people buy junk food with food stamps. What do
they know about beans and meat? They know what they see
on television, in the magazines; they know the Mercedes
they see *him* driving. Your capitalism, she wanted to say, is
educating them in desperate ignorance. Your free enterprise
system.

She did not say any of it.

Her first husband would be thinking and maybe saying
these things. He would know that the people around the
table were the enemy, the very same she and he had fought
when they lived in Chicago and worked against the war in
Vietnam. The same they had studied during the terrible six-
ties, the same they had hated.

"You're so quiet," her husband said, leaning toward her,
giving her his hand. He was handsome and gentle and he
didn't pontificate like his father, and she loved him in spite of
a score of things and for a hundred others: not the least of
them his stability, his good sense, his ability to be socially at
ease with people, his open affection with her, the pure security of him.

"I was wondering," she said, "about the carving around
this table." She tried to say it quietly, so the rest wouldn't

hear. "I know one of the wooden scallops was added, because one was broken, and I've been trying to guess if any of
these," and she ran her hand along the perimeter of the table,
"is the new one. To see if it really fits so well."

"None have been added," he said. He seemed confused.

"You told me one was new. I remember."

"Nan's right," his father said. "One is new. I can't find it,
either."

The other daughter-in-law and the mother had begun to
play backgammon. They used an inlaid, ebony board and
when the dice were thrown they clicked like teeth. Her husband's brother had taken out an expensive cigar and was
lighting it with great ceremony. He looked rich. His haircut
looked rich and exactly right, and his three-piece suit matched
his shirt and tie exactly. He had a bored rich face and a
sullen lower lip. You could not ask him a question because
he would never answer it; he made light of everything.

The mother-in-law was beautiful and smooth skinned, and
Nan had often watched her play with the grandchildren. She
was the best of them all, but even in the best there was this
other thing. In one game, the woman lined the grandchildren
up to race. When they were ready, she broke before she'd
finished counting—she always won. One grandchild had
cried the first time she did it. "Grandmother lies," she'd said,
laughing. The next time, the child who cried—a little girl—
broke away early too.

Her first husband would have seen and understood all
this, and although she didn't love him and didn't miss him,
she respected his intelligence and he was more like her,
shared with her a way of seeing. He would have observed
her new husband's expensive suit, and her own diamond, and
her own good haircut. But he's gone, she thought, and
that's over. She released her new husband's hand. I'm seeing
with my own eyes, she thought, and I mustn't blame it on
anyone else. So now I must decide what to do.

COASTAL

Katherine was Midwestern and had been sent East by her Uncle Richard, who in 1967, when she was sixteen, had proposed financing her education.

That night they were in her parents' kitchen, and june bugs beat against the screens. Uncle Richard wore an imported silk suit, soft Italian shoes, a pink rose in his lapel. Since she was a little girl he had always sent her gifts from places whose names she could not pronounce: strange packages, dusty gray tissue paper. Her family knew little about his private life, except that he traveled. And that he looked nothing like his brother, her father, who was wearing a white, short-sleeved sports shirt and permanent-press slacks, and so foreign beside her mother in her cotton housedress. Her parents had never left Ohio.

Uncle Richard tapped his fingers on the Formica table. He said Katherine was sensitive, precocious, deserving. He took the flower from his lapel, leaned across to her, and put it in her hair. *I'll never have children of my own*, he said. *I want to do this*. Katherine thought of school, her friends going to movies and ice skating—they would stay in Jamesville forever. That night she fell asleep with the flower softening in her hand, and its limp petals lay between the sheets in the morning.

She met Drew, her husband, while she was a senior honors' student at Bard; married him two years later on the flagstone terrace outside his parents' house, overlooking the harbor where his father's yacht was moored. Light fragmented from the rigging of the boats and reached the party like fugitive signals, a mute, formal code of desperation. But desperation at a distance is silent, remote. At the wedding the guests mistook Uncle Richard for her own father. She was pleased, then ashamed, then proud.

Afterward she worked as a historian at the town museum, entertained Drew's friends, shopped with his mother, waxed the antique lowboy that had been their wedding gift. Uncle Richard went away on a tour to Iceland. He sent a postcard telling about the silence of glaciers. *They are the color of your eyes, my dear,* he said, *that blue.* After a year and a half in Jones Harbor, she came to see the undulating shape of the town spread along the ocean like the skirts of a woman drunk at a party, a woman who is still trying when she should have stopped. Jones Harbor was a dowager, Katherine decided. One didn't know whether to praise her or be embarrassed for her—one couldn't decide if the proper word was courage. And also, Katherine saw the glorious streaked sunsets over the mudflats and the tidal river. She saw the melting ice in Drew's evening drinks. She saw the oil paintings at his parents' house; the enduring, indifferent granite of expensive coastal properties; the vapid photographs of trips to the Virgin Islands, the Bahamas. And she drank gin and tonic under green and yellow canvas umbrellas at a private club. Jones Harbor exhausted her. Yet it began to seem that she could continue living as she was for years and years, a sleepwalker. She knew that she had stopped hearing people, had stopped paying attention. Maybe she was in danger, but she couldn't name the threat.

In July of the second summer, she was off work early and decided to drive to the marina. The sky was clear lapis blue, and the sailboat masts made firm rows. When she first met Drew, she had been ignorant about boats. Now she knew enough to name their parts, to tell a ketch from a yawl. She

knew how to tie a bowline. And she had a sense of the indi-
vidual character of boats. Some were elegant, some merely
utilitarian, some high sided and ugly; the good ones were
mysterious and promised adventure. The very best ones
promised grace.

She parked the car and walked along a row of hauled-out
sailboats standing in their cradles. At the end of the row, just
before the dock ramp, the last boat was a daysailer. She
stopped to look at it, leaning with her elbows on the rails. It
was a bewitching boat. Across the tidy hull, she looked out
to the harbor and the large boats moored there, turning
gently in the tide.

When she had been alone with the boat a long time, a
man came out to speak with her. By then she had run her
hands along the generous outward curve of the hull; she had
calculated the money Uncle Richard had given her for a
wedding present. The man talked confidingly of cost and
terms. He said the boat was a Herreshoff. She had heard the
name before. He said the design was classic. Katherine asked
only a few questions: Did a trailer come with the boat? Could
she get a mooring? Inside, in an office that smelled of oil-
based paint and rubber, while a mongrel dog sniffed absently
at her feet, she wrote a check to hold the boat, and signed.

The Herreshoff was the most lovely boat she had ever
seen. Its rails were varnished maghogany; all the fittings
were silky brass. The decks were covered with white canvas.
The hull was white and beautifully sanded, glossy. It took
many thin coats of paint to produce such a finish. The boat
had green sail covers for the mainsail and jib; enough space
under its bench seats to store life jackets and water; room
enough for two adults, or an adult and two children. It was a
perfect, scaled-down version of a large yacht: a filly among
stallions.

A wood boat is too much work, Drew said. You need a

mooring every year. It's so deep keeled, the marina will have
to haul it out. If you'd asked me, I'd have said get a center-
board boat. You'll unload it by next summer. But Katherine
did not want to think about next summer. She named the
boat *Coastal*. She liked the sound of the word: light air offshore, gentle weather. Silence like a Hopper painting.

All that summer, she realized, she had been thinking of
Ohio. There had been a stream behind their house, and she'd
kept a punky old rowboat in it. When she was small she
used to lead the boat through the water by the bowline pre-
tending it was a horse. Then she put oars in the locks and
taught herself to row, bailing the flat bottom with an old
coffee can. Iridescent blue-and-green flies landed on the
chipped wood. Over the sound of water slapping, she remembered hearing her mother's voice calling her in for
lunch. A voice in place, as the boat was in place, as the
summer day was. She had been happy then.

The last Saturday in August, Drew was sailing in a day
race with his friend Ken Perkins. The weather was sticky
hot, but she drove down to watch them get underway. Perkins's boat was imported from Sweden, sheer and low, rigged
for racing. The hull was green and swift looking. She waved
to them from the dock, though already they weren't watching. Back at home she swept the kitchen floor and put a load
into the washing machine. Then she stood at the dining room
window and looked at the dry lawn.

Finally, at noon, when a sea breeze came up, she packed a
lunch and went down to the marina. The causeway shim-
mered; the heat was confining. In the car mirror she pursed
her mouth and saw how tight her skin was. Above the
sunglasses, there were faint lines between her eyes like her
mother's.

Drew had sailed with her in the Herreshoff three times,
but she had never taken the boat out alone. At the moor-

ing, she checked for life jackets and stowed the thermos of
orange juice, the sandwich, and potato chips, under the fore-
deck. Then she primed the three-horse outboard. It finally
came alive after five tries with the rope. The rope was dirty
and grease came off on her hands. She let the engine idle
while she tied Drew's skiff to the mooring line and cast
off. She had to zigzag past moored boats to get out of the
harbor. They had grand names: *Dawn Piper*, *Showdown*,
Harrier.

In the channel she was passed by two large sailboats heading out. People on board waved with the lazy, indifferent
camaraderie of sailors. A woman wearing a khaki hat waved
hard and for a long time, until Katherine turned away and
looked out toward the ledges and the black channel marker.
Blue and yellow lobster buoys were pulling in the tide.

The ocean was pewter, with rolling swells. Even away
from the heat of land, the skin of the water looked hot to
touch, and there was a haze far out; in it she could see the
tall, white mainsail of a very large boat. She motored a while
and then let the boat drift in idle, heading into the light air,
while she removed the sail covers and set the main.

When the jib was raised, and she had turned off the engine, when she had fallen into the perfect quiet of a sailboat
as the sails fill with air, she realized that she had brought the
feeling with her. She looked at the Dacron sails, gently taut
now. The wind, she guessed, was blowing about seven knots.
She looked at the telltales, bits of red yarn tied to the stays.
Her feeling was an emptiness, more profound than simple
boredom, and she regretted. Why couldn't it be easy, just to
go out of the harbor and forget? Drew had said this always
happened to him. In a race, as he was now, everything was
business: the most efficient tack, the best trim for the sails.
Ken had a crew of college boys—one for each sail. It would
be a slow race, and Drew would not be home until late. He
was doing what he loved.

But, even loving, he was unconscious of it. He didn't think. He went to boats the way a retriever goes for a stick.

She listened to the water slapping under the bow and decided that in order to enjoy the day she needed to have a destination, though all targets seemed arbitrary, so she chose Heron Island, six miles offshore. The wind seemed to carry her in that direction.

She thought of Ohio. She had never sailed in Ohio, though some people did on Lake Erie. Ohio was her grandmother's blue plate over the farmhouse sink; it was family reunions with tables spread out beside the great lilac bushes. It was a box elder tree. It was flat land, checkerboard town streets, space in fields almost like the space of the ocean, like the space she felt within herself now. Packed in a closet now, she had photographs of herself: a six-year-old girl holding a barn cat. But also in the closet: postcards from Uncle Richard.

She concentrated on the boat. Holding the varnished tiller, she ran her free hand along the smooth combing. She examined and tested the brass turnbuckles for tightness and secure fastening. She checked the lines and found them supple.

It was a lovely, bright boat; it moved cheerfully. Around midafternoon, when the breeze picked up, the boat skidded through the water, heeled over, and she felt momentarily a heady sense of freedom. Perhaps she would not have to go back, but would head up toward the Maine coast and put in somewhere at sunset. Drew would have to come and get her. If she went ashore and phoned.

All afternoon, she tried to draw closer to Heron Island, but although she stayed on course the island still hung in the distance. Without question she was farther from shore. Three miles out anyway, she imagined, maybe four. She could see the dark line of trees on the mainland and the occasional white smudge of a large house. Across the vacant ocean she could see other, large sailboats far off.

Around five o'clock, the wind died. For a while she sat

quietly, feeling the Herreshoff rocking in the swells. She took out her sandwich and ate it, feeling queasy, and drank some orange juice. It would not do to start the engine at once; a real sailor waited a while, preferring to sail home. But the wind did not come up again. In the distance she saw a red buoy—maybe the one outside the harbor entrance. She was too far away to be sure.

Finally she decided to motor back. She primed the engine and pulled on the dirty cord two, three times. Her arm ached. She heard the familiar grinding, but the engine did not catch. Once it almost did, and she held her breath, but then it died again. That was the fourth try. Afterward, she smelled gasoline, and the engine was simply dead. Flooded. She pushed in the choke and rested for what seemed twenty minutes, but which she later thought was only three or four, and pulled again. The cord stuck and then gave; it broke under her hand.

She sat back and looked out over the water. Boats were along shore now, going in to port. *It won't do to panic*, she thought. Panicking.

When the sun went down she had wearied herself with trying to get into the engine and somehow replace the cord with extra line; she had set the sails over again but there was no wind to fill them; she had thought of Drew coming home, finding her gone, going to the marina and seeing the skiff on the mooring, borrowing a powerboat and coming to look for her—she had rejected the possibility. He would not get in until nine or ten; it would be too late, by then, to find her. The Herreshoff had no running lights. She listened to the mainsail flapping, and the boom swung back and forth as the boat rocked. Everything on the boat seemed to be in motion, to click and creak against something else. There was no wind at all. Finally she lowered the jib and rolled it up. Her foot slipped on the deck and she clutched the mast. She sat in the cockpit and waited until she could breathe evenly. Then she lowered the main, too, and fastened the boom in its cradle. She tied the tiller.

Darkness came very fast now, and the sky was thinly red along the horizon. She leaned against the transom, sat up again. She crawled forward and reached under the deck for the thermos of orange juice. She'd been casual with it and there was only a third left—a bit more than a cup. So she wet her mouth and closed the thermos again tightly. A pale, humid moon was rising, and she could see two stars.

Her throat was dry from fear. She imagined herself doing impossible things, jumping from the boat and swimming home—it was only a few miles. She imagined having a telephone on board. Or a fishing boat coming up quickly to tow her, like a rescue in a television movie; but when she looked around there was no boat nearby, and the one with running lights near shore was too far away to see her.

There are times you go back, she was thinking. Uncle Richard was good and he had adored her, but he was a dreamer. You go back past pink roses and lace sundresses, and postcards from exotic places, because these things are flimsy. You go back past patios and antiques and oil paintings in the entry hall. Then what do you have?

Her father had told her a hunting story once. He was in Michigan, far into the north woods with four friends. They were staying at a camp. During the night there was a dusting of snow and they got out early to look for deer. Somehow he was separated from the rest of the party, and—he said—he kept walking, his first mistake, until he came across his own footprints in the snow. In a low, confiding voice he told her that he had been afraid. His face was tense from embarrassment. He was so frightened, he said, that he wouldn't walk, and he sat down and leaned against a tree. Very late, when they found him with flashlights, shouting, he said they might as well not have come because he had learned something he could not unlearn afterward: that he was alone and there was nothing to be done. "Don't tell your mother," he had said. "I don't want her ever to know."

Katherine stood up and yelled toward shore for help; it was foolish, but she couldn't stop. She sat again, her face hot, her throat sore from yelling, and then leaned and vomited over the rail. Finally, when she vomited dryly, she raised her head and hit her fist on the canvas deck.

During the night she slipped between dreaming and waking, not always able to tell which was dream: she was standing in line at a market behind a poor woman with a handful of food coupons, and the woman had lines between her eyes like her mother's, and she, Katherine, turned her diamond ring inward against her palm. She was talking to Drew, who switched on the television in the middle of her sentence. She was phoning her mother but the phone was not answered.

Awake, she lay on the wood cockpit grate and listened to the water slapping and looked at the sky. The wood combing was wet from dew. The small of her back was stiff and one elbow hurt where she'd bumped the transom. A halyard flung sideways when the boat took an odd wave; she stood and made the halyard fast. Very late, she thought, "I'm a damned fool not to have a pillow." And she pressed the folded life jacket under her head. She swirled a small mouthful of orange juice against her teeth, and it burned as it ran down her throat. *There's enough*, she thought. *Just enough*. She imagined Drew in from racing, putting the boat to bed and going home; and upstairs, brushing his teeth, washing, using the toilet and going to their room. She saw him curled up and snoring—was it possible?

Then she slept a long time, an hour or more, and woke feeling shaky and chilled but somehow rested. The ocean was black, rolling. The boat creaked gently. A few thin clouds spun around the moon; the sky had cleared. She heard her-

self groan, and she gripped the combing and longed for what
she had not done; not brought the transistor weather radio,
not left a note saying where she was going, not brought
water, nor a warm sweater, nor even a flashlight. Someone
else had always taken care of such things. She did not even
know, now, where the tide carried her.

Toward dawn, she touched the boat—the smooth wood.
She loosened the tiller and, holding it, let the boat have its
gentle motion. Half-standing, she put her hand into the cold
water. The sky lightened.

*   *   *

Drew was on board the Coast Guard cutter; she recog-
nized his sailing hat and dark glasses. The boat pulled near,
large and white, a red chevron on its hull. It broke the waves
apart. They were so close now that she could see Drew's
face; he looked serious, and his mouth was partly open. He
scratched the back of his head and his shoulders slumped. A
young sailor threw her a line, and she made it fast to a cleat
on the bow. But when he motioned to pull her alongside and
take her aboard, she shook her head no. She wanted to hold
the tiller herself.

It was only forty-five minutes to the marina. They towed
her in the spreading wake at a moderate speed—the Herreshoff was so small—and she tried to work out an explanation. But there was no explanation. She thought of what she
might tell Drew, but there was nothing. She looked at the
furling water under the bow. It was shocking how much she
loved this boat.

As they entered the mouth of the channel, five men on the
deck of the cutter watched her, talking among themselves.
One opened his arms widely, as if making a joke about catch-
ing a big fish. Drew moved over to join them. He bent his
head to light a cigarette.

Would they sit at dinner tonight and talk it over? She knew

they would not. It would not be discussed, this adventure, this rescue: it would be a faux pas, and she was a naughty girl who had embarrassed him. Never mind that the tiller was solid in her hand. Drew would pour the wine and they would drink. Perhaps they would watch television before bed. Then they would go upstairs, separate as two planets. She knew it and she saw it—the way she knew the Herreshoff now, the way she saw every wave breaking on the ledges.

LIKE BOATS

Almost every night after work Peter went to the Harbor Bar. Often the woman with the hat was there, and he watched her. She usually sat with two friends at one of the low, round tables beside the bay windows. The bar was downstairs, so the windows looked out at the road; beyond the road were summer houses, then cliffs, then the ocean. It was part of an inn, an old summer residence. You could not see the ocean from Harbor Bar but, as with all places along the seacoast route, you could feel it: empty, vast, prescient.

He guessed that she was about his age, near forty. Her funny white hat had a brim that flopped down over her dark eyes, and she used a cigarette holder. When she was laughing—and she laughed often—her face changed. She had a long face, until then. He couldn't tell what color her hair was in the dim light; it was dark, he hoped it was auburn.

Peter always chose exactly the same place at the far end of the long row of bar stools, to wait for Josh. They were both lawyers and this was the bar where professionals hung out. Behind the row of men gathered after five o'clock one could picture kids and women, dinner kept warm on kitchen stoves until the vegetables were soft and unpalatable and the meat was gray and overdone, and every man that Peter knew in the bar, every friend he met there, had reasons for staying. Reasons, Peter thought now, excuses and reasons, were the mortar and stone of the foundation of a place like Harbor Bar—tucked in among summerhouses, a period house itself, renovated for the public. There was a small, carved wooden sign over the door outside, but the inn didn't need to advertise.

The woman with the white hat wore becoming trim suits, low pumps, silk blouses. Tonight her blouse was peach colored. He guessed that she worked in town or maybe in the next town. Somehow she had found this bar and obviously liked it; she was often there. It would have been easy to ask somebody who she was, but he hadn't done that.

His wedding band clicked against the highball glass when he picked it up. A thick gold band: when he and Jenny were arguing, he twirled the ring around on his finger. Last week it had rolled right off and landed with a crack on the pegged wood floor at home. Two months after they were married, six years ago now, the band had broken. A flaw in the metal, the jeweler said. Jenny had wanted to buy him a new ring, but he said he wanted the ring he was married in. She said it was bad luck. Nonsense, he said. He was uncomfortable now, living with Jenny, with the way he felt living with her. He pictured Jenny cooking, her face tense; Jenny wondering where he had been and why he was late, dinner was cold; asking him to spend part of the weekend in the garden when he wanted to fix the winches on the sloop; Jenny telling him he needed a physical checkup, a haircut, to see more of Danny and less of Josh. When they were first married he used to drive off to work thinking of how her skin felt, how her eyes were. Now in the morning he rolled out of bed without kissing her; he avoided her face that was blurry from sleep; he went into the bathroom and brushed his teeth and refused to think about why.

He leaned forward on the bar stool and loosened his tie. He thought of Jenny looking out the kitchen window for him into the dark—for it was still dark early—and he hunched up his shoulders, shrugged them down. Dinner kept warm.

He liked this spot in the bar: the smooth mahogany, worn

along the edge from hands. He could turn and lean against the dark, paneled wall and watch the front door. He liked the scotch and water they mixed for him, nice scotch, mixed strong. He liked to twirl his finger around in the drink and push the ice cubes in a spiral. He liked to touch his liquor. Sometimes when he lifted the glass to drink he kept his index finger there so he could feel the cold against his skin as well as in his mouth. And then that nice, smoky bite. It cleared his palate. After two or three drinks, it settled his mind.

The waitress with the sooty black hair was leaning against the other end of the bar, smoking a cigarette. She and the owner were lovers, somebody had said. She had a hard, tense body and she was not as young as she looked in the dark; her black skirt was tight and too short. The owner was playing bartender tonight and he stood against the sinks with his arms folded. To Peter they both seemed to be waiting: the waitress to look at the owner through the veil of her cigarette smoke, the owner to unfold his arms.

Peter looked over to the window table where the woman with the hat was sitting with one of her friends. She was wearing a light gray suit tonight. The hat was out of place with the suit. He guessed that she put it on after work; it was her off-hours hat, almost a costume. She had a thin gold bracelet, and a ring with a stone. She didn't seem to notice that he was watching her. He wondered how her hands felt to touch, whether they were warm or cool.

He touched his drink. The glass was cool. When Josh came they could talk and he could keep on looking over Josh's shoulder. This was the first time, he realized, that he actually planned to watch her, the first time he had conscious intent.

The door opened and Josh came in, his big shoulders filling the entryway. Josh had just finished his bar exams; he was a researcher for a firm in town. He was wearing a suit.

To Jenny and Peter's wedding, Josh had worn a denim jacket
with a dragon embroidered on the back. Probably he was
being insulting because his own marriage had just ended.
Lots of people in town, Jenny included, didn't like Josh, but
Peter did. They'd known each other since they were kids—
Peter took him in stride. Josh had flunked the bar exams the
first time, but Peter didn't care about that. He liked to sail
with Josh. Every spring they worked together on Peter's
Cape Dory, and every summer they cruised alone for a week
Down East. On the boat they often worked side by side
without speaking; he put out his hand and Josh put the
right-sized wrench in it. When they were both single, twice
they had slept with the same woman. They didn't discuss it
afterward, though they both knew. It was a felt thing, a look
in the eyes, a grin.

Nice night, Josh said, looking around the bar.

It was almost spring. When the door to Harbor Bar was
opened, Peter could almost hear the ocean out there—the
groaning buoy off the harbor entrance, the lighthouse on the
breakwater. Almost spring and then, by God, summer; they
would have to get working on the boat. They? He and Jenny.
No: he and Josh.

Not much tonight, Josh said. He turned back to Peter.
Empty place. What's new?

Peter shrugged.

Summer's coming, Josh said.

I was just thinking that.

So we have to sand the keel, Josh said.

The waitress had put out her cigarette and she was turned
now to survey the bar, one hand on her hip. She winked
affectedly at Josh. She looked old. She looked so old it made
Peter feel sick.

The woman with the white hat stood up as her friend was
leaving; then she sat back down again alone with her back

to the window. Her tall drink was half gone. She was facing
him but not looking at him. Over Josh's bulky shoulders,
Peter watched her, and to amuse himself he made up a life
for her: she had a decent salary—maybe $25,000 a year—
and a secretary. She sold real estate. No: she owned a real
estate business. Or she was a bank manager. Or she was
office manager with one of the big companies down in Ports-
mouth. She liked to come to Harbor Bar for the same reasons that he did: it was downstairs, private, and you could
talk without people hassling you. He wondered if, for weeks
now, she had been watching him. He flattered himself that it
was true. He was the one who always sat at the end of the
bar and she liked his face and his big square hands and she
wondered about his hands.

He motioned to the bartender with two fingers for drinks.

Took Mona home last night, Josh said. Stayed until three
A.M. I'm beat today.

Fine, Peter said. Terrific.

The bartender brought them both fresh drinks, and Peter put his finger in the glass again, twirled the ice cubes.
The woman with the hat had taken a folder from her brief-
case and was looking through a set of bound papers that
appeared to be a report. The hat was pulled down and he
couldn't see her eyes; she was turned so that beside the table
her legs stretched out long and smooth. He looked at her
legs, and for a moment they made him want to weep.

Look but don't touch, Josh said.

Christ, Peter said.

You're a barrel of laughs tonight, Peter, Josh said.

Peter was thinking about the time last summer when he
and Josh were underway in the boat late in the afternoon in
fog—it was so thick and greasy you couldn't see thirty feet.
They were looking for the entrance to Seal Cove so they
could put in for the night. It had been a bright fog, so they

knew the bank wasn't high and had plenty of sun above it, but the fog was thick over the water. Josh was on the bow and Peter was at the wheel. The engine was cut back so low he could hear water sloshing against the hull. They seemed to be spinning in circles in the fog. In spite of all his time at sea, as darkness came on, Peter had felt the tight beginnings of despair. And then Josh had pointed, just as the fog lifted slightly, and before them were the lights of a harbor a mile off. When he looked at it, he couldn't breathe. They got their bearings and slid easily in. It was one of the times he and Josh didn't have to speak. That night the water in Seal Cove was so unusually warm they jumped in before dinner to swim, laughing like thieves.

For a long time he looked into his drink glass. There was a good sea running now, from yesterday's storm; the beaches would be full of kelp and their friend Curly would be looking through the kelp for hen clams—Curly always did that after a storm, brought the fat bastards home and chopped the meat and made baked stuffed clams. You could count on it—Curly was like clockwork; he was like the sun coming up. It made Peter happy, briefly, to think of old Curly on the beach in his black rubber boots picking up hen clams. He had wanted a life like that himself: things you could know and count on, all the time, no matter what. Curly lived with his mother still, though he was forty-two. Curly and his mother were almost like husband and wife; she worried, he took off.

Curly's probably on the beach now, Peter said.

Josh smiled. Tide's right, isn't it.

Goddamned Curly, Peter said.

We'll get him up to deer camp this year.

Sure, and his mother'll throw fits.

He'll go anyway, Josh said. Always does.

Curly had said he felt uncomfortable around Jenny. Peter

thought of her sad eyes and then he made himself stop it. He could not, he realized, imagine the next day. Not the next month, never mind years. The years floated away like boats into fog: her face at the kitchen window when he got out of the car to come in, guilt falling on him silently like a thick coat.

That's it, Josh said. He set down his empty glass and buttoned his jacket. See you next time.

Peter didn't want him to leave, but he didn't say anything. He held his glass tighter. For a minute, Josh's leaving tugged at him with a feeling almost like pain; he watched Josh's back as he headed toward the door, as he stopped to tease the waitress. She touched his arm and he grinned at her. Then he was gone.

Peter motioned for another scotch. When he looked around, the woman with the white hat was smiling at him. She was waiting there, it seemed, like a destination, a target, like the lights of Seal Cove, as he crossed the room with the drink in his hand.

MERCY FLIGHTS

Bill Troolin is flying a missionary plane into wild areas of Mexico to deliver food and supplies and to rescue sick people. He has a wife named Bridgette and two children: Donny, aged five, and Tooter, aged one-and-a-half. Bill Troolin was the farm kid with the gorgeous dark hair and the lovely cheekbones; the shy boy with the strong, tenor voice; the kid who had one girlfriend all through high school. He was the boy I sat with on the senior hayride and we gently necked a little while, and I thought then, as I have thought about other people a few times since, "I could fall in love right now." And didn't. The draft horses were pulling steadily along the hard gravel road and the trailer bed smelled of horses and hay. We were going around Spectacle Lake. I leaned back in the moonlight and chill September air, and the possibility of love with Bill Troolin was as simple as a shutter closing over the eye of a camera, a wing of cloud brushing the moon.

In another part of the wagon Dwayne Norstad lit an illegal cigarette and Karin Curtis laughed, a trilling high laugh that was excited and embarrassed at the same time. Two nights before, Karin and I had been babysitting and sneaking Camel cigarettes from the cupboard, smoking them quickly in the downstairs bathroom. Then we made ourselves cups of thick grainy coffee and practiced drinking it with cigarettes in our hands. Karin and Dwayne were going steady. She wore his class ring—a heavy thing with a garish red stone—on a chain around her neck. Or she

wound the back with surgical adhesive so she could wear it
on her finger. I wanted very much to go steady with somebody, but the boy I dated was from Oconomowoc, Wiscon-
sin, and I only saw him every few weeks. He didn't buy a
class ring, he said, because it would get banged up when he
worked on his motorcycle. That small decision of Michael's
set a rippling sadness going in me; I think I never forgave
him for it. He may have been lying; another girl may have
had his ring; I never found out. I don't know if he still has
a motorcycle. Or if he has become a banker, an engineer. I
know this: he isn't flying missionary planes or making res-
cues. Not Michael.

That night Bill Troolin and I, who had often during choir
rehearsal eyed each other over the sheet music, happened
to be in the same area of flatbed trailer sharing a spot of
straw. He put his arm under my shoulders and I could feel
his hard, knotty muscles. His skin was warm. I relaxed all
down my body; I even yawned. Then, feeling silly, I leaned
on my elbows to watch the dark trees just as our wagon
passed the dirt side road where, only two weeks before,
Paul Johanson had gone in his pin-striped Chevy with a
bottle of blackberry brandy and a twelve-gauge shotgun,
drove down the road a mile and parked the car, got out, sat
down against a tree, and shot himself in the head. The police found the bottle half empty, and Paul had forgotten to
turn the Chevy off. The battery was dead and they had to
charge it to get the car out of the woods. Not so with his
body, which they covered with a sheet as neatly as a bunk-
bed at summer camp. Paul was, like us, a high school senior, and nobody knew him very well—which is a quote
from the newspaper. The week after he killed himself, Karin and Janice and Lori and I all seemed in our own ways
to fall in love with him: a reflexive, urgent emotion. We
talked about his long legs, his ambling walk. We wondered

if he had ever had a girl. Whatever we felt, it was over by
Saturday and afterward we spoke of him in superstitious
voices; the mention of Paul Johanson seemed to be an invi-
tation for trouble to enter our lives.

I looked at Bill Troolin to see if he knew what I was
thinking, but I couldn't see his face. And on the wagon,
everyone was silent.

In another two weeks we'd have our first choir concert of
the season. We'd sing "In The Still Of The Night." There
was no moon on the rim of the hill for us, since there was
no hill: that part of Minnesota is flat from glaciation. When
I sang, the rim of the hill was like the edge of a cup into
which a lozenge-shaped moon dropped after balancing for
endless moments. Then, I thought, something splendid and
nameless would happen; what happened, happened forever,
and the best part was that you knew it.

Bill Troolin put his smooth cheek against my face. His
skin was exquisite; when I breathed I seemed to inhale it.
This was the only time I would ever be touched by him,
Baptist then, missionary now. I thought then of Bill immersed at his baptism, and, being Lutheran, I began to
laugh. He pulled back and looked at me, but it was too
dark to see his eyes. "Never mind," I said. "It's nothing."
But still I held the picture of him in white, flowing robes
that swirled in the water like weeds, and his grand hair was
matted to his skull, and a look of beatific rapture was on
his fine-boned face, and the minister hauled off and lowered
him into the water—bubbles coming up?—and the words
of the Bible were spoken, and the whole congregation
raised hands together to praise the Lord.

We Lutherans hated the Baptists and thought them fairly
pagan, embarrassing. When I imagined the bubbles I laughed
again, and he turned away. It didn't seem possible that I
could hurt Bill Troolin—we hardly knew each other—but I

put my hand on his arm anyhow, and stroked it against the grain of fine dark hair. I was thinking of lines from a poem we had memorized in English class:

Ah, love, let us be true
To one another!

*   *   *

I live alone now, and take weekend walks along the ocean with my dog. It's June, and the sidewalk is lined with harsh, lovely, tough sea roses that die within a few minutes if you pick them. Some are rose and some are white; in late season the petals scatter and knobby rose hips grow luminously where the flowers have been. Below the sidewalk is Seal Beach, not popular among tourists because it's gone at high tide; and I go down to that beach and run until my legs ache and I can't take a full breath, the dog loping easily beside me on the sand. The dog runs with a ball in its mouth. My husband, who has been gone two months and lives in another part of town, wanted a hunting dog one year.

When Andrew was first gone, the dog waited at the door every night for him and I watched the dog watching.

One night I burned my wrist when I poured boiling water into the drip pot. The steam blanketed my arm and I jumped backward; for a minute my vision went black, and I turned reflexively to the refrigerator. Then I went to the orange chair and held the ice cube to my wrist. The radio was going as if nothing had happened and the dog was standing near me. The house was as empty as if the dog and I had not been in it.

I stretched my legs out and took deep breaths, and still I couldn't get rid of the weight on my chest. Perhaps, I thought, I will be an old woman alone and this will happen. Perhaps something else will happen.

Some weeks later, when the burn was a scarred welt, I cut
the index finger on that same hand while I was slicing vegetables. It was just growing dark outside, and I looked at the
blood traveling around my knuckle in its neat, bright track,
dripping on the maple board. It was a deep cut and it bled
profusely. I stood there looking outward at the trees I have
loved for years, at the grass that needed mowing, at the per-
ennials bed that I would mulch over that weekend. The
blood fell in drops among the peppers and onions. It just
kept on. I didn't move.

He would not help me. He would not be anywhere nearby;
he was not coming back. My hand was my hand, my wrist
my wrist. And then at once the fear left and something worse
replaced it: I was fascinated, enthralled. Colors spun on the
maple board—green, red, the translucent pearly white of
onions. Onions in rounds, peppers in chunks. They were
fluid and mobile and I loved them. But something caution-
ary, like a voice inside me or a hand on my shoulder, made
me stop it and I reached for the cold-water faucet and put
my fingers under it. When the bleeding had slowed, I wrapped
the finger in a paper towel and went upstairs for a bandage.
My back was cold; the back of my neck was stiff. I was
shaking. After that, I began walking the dog every night on
the leash no matter how tired I was.

This Saturday, I went to Seal Beach early as I often do on
weekends. Across the beach I saw a red-haired man and a
little girl. I had intended to run, so I pulled down my sleeves
and ran half the length of the sand in his direction—it was
the only direction—and when I stopped to get my breath we
were a hundred yards apart. I could see his face. He had
been watching me. There was, even at distance, a loneliness
about him. It even seemed that the energy of his loneliness,
and that of my own, made an arc between us. His little girl
was playing in the edge of surf; she skipped on the glassy

pulling water, and in the early sunlight it shot up like sparks around her feet. Then she ran toward us.

I was walking toward them now.

"That's a pretty dog," she said. She was drawing a large circle in the sand with her foot.

I looked at them both from under the brim of my hat. She had red hair too, but a more delicate mouth.

The girl stepped into the center of her circle. "Nobody can come in!" she said. "This is mine!"

I guessed she was seven or eight. The man looked at her, then at me. He was wearing a short-sleeved plaid shirt, and he had sinewy arms. "Do you live around here?" he said. His voice was husky, unused.

As if I wanted to please him, I turned and pointed toward the road that went up along the granite and disappeared behind a row of summerhouses, and my sleeves fell back along my wrists showing the scar. He pointed the other way, off toward the lighthouse, to a chocolate-colored Cape Cod with a slate roof. He said his family had bought that summer house thirty years ago. He still came up from Massachusetts every season. When he was first summering there, he said, there were only a few houses and you could see clear off to Kennebunkport where, at night, lights curved along the edge of the ocean like a string of stones on a bracelet. Then he appeared surprised at what he had said. My dog was chasing seagulls along the water and we all turned to watch her. I felt embarrassed, the way a kid does in a movie when the lovers are kissing bigger than life on the screen. I felt like moving closer to him. Then I thought of my husband, and wondered where he was this minute, what he was thinking of, whether he was happy with what he'd done. *Don't*, I said in my mind. I looked again at the man and the girl and thought, *Where's your wife now? Where's your mother?*

"What's your dog's name?" the girl said.

We were standing on the ragged, sandy edges of the girl's circle. She was wearing a navy chamois shirt and blue jeans, and her hair was dark auburn, in braids. There's a picture of me when I was eight, holding a barn cat in front of my uncle's house, my hair in braids. She put her hands on her hips and looked at us.

You can smell divorce. It makes folks run away, even those who are themselves divorcing. The only ones who don't run are those in singles bars at night, so mulled on booze that any lonely creature looks like a target, because in the high illusion and noise of a bar it's possible to imagine an exciting, impossible world that shatters every morning, that takes real work to recreate every evening, until finally the work of construction is so exhausting you don't bother any longer.

I'd been working hard all summer at the office so that I would barely think at night; only shop for groceries, do laundry, exercise the dog, sink into bed with enough reading to last a week of nights.

I told the girl my dog's name. The red-haired man asked if I came here often, and I said I did. My breath was even now. I was coming down off the running, and I was able to look at his face. He had a good, warm face; it must have been an open face, when he was a boy. He looked nothing at all like my husband. *I could fall in love right now*, I was thinking. Then I might show him my scar, and tell him, perhaps, that I was barely alive when it happened.

I pulled my sleeves down and straightened my hat. The girl dragged her toe in the sand in the center of her circle, making wet *X*'s.

We had nothing to say. I looked in the direction that he had pointed. He looked where I had pointed. Then we began simultaneously to laugh; our arms had been crossing in the lines that they made, and the distance between the two points was infinity.

"There!" he said.

"No, there!" I said.

The girl threw up her arms in the middle of her circle like the conductor at a complicated modern symphony, and my dog came back panting.

I began to run again, the rest of the length of the beach, and I felt the man grow smaller behind me and I didn't look back. Ahead, coming closer, were the summerhouses perched on the edge of granite with their dreamy, open porches looking out at the open ocean, with their rows of expectant deck chairs and beds of lemon lilies and pots of scarlet geraniums. The sky was as blue as a Chinese bowl tipped over—empty as a bowl—and the humid air was substantial, as though one breathed it in dense mouthfuls. When I reached the far end of the beach I bent and stretched, my hands on my knees. I stood up again and turned around; he was leaving. His daughter was watching me too, and they both waved at me. It was such a kind gesture that I pulled off my hat and waved back. A piece of hair blew across my forehead and into my eyes. Of course they couldn't see I was crying.

*　　*　　*

The news about Bill Troolin's missionary flights was in this morning's mail, part of a list of classmates for my fifteenth class reunion. Some of the most unmemorable people were doing the most interesting things. I poured coffee and made a bowl of mixed fruit and read the list: Delmar photographing Eskimos, Janice with the foreign service in Guatemala, Shirley teaching forestry at the University of Vermont, Jimmy consulting for industry in Connecticut. Through the kitchen window I saw the ocean and one working lobster boat; through the French doors I heard the throaty diesel engine. A flock of gulls spun around the stern, only a few feet up, waiting for old bait.

Every friend I had was on that hayride: Karin and Dwayne and Janice and Dougie and Lori and Steve and Ramona and Carl. There were other flatbed wagons pulled by horses behind us, a convoy of them—five. When we started, the sun was just going down and light was pink behind the black pines. It was too cold by then for swimming. But all summer long we'd been swimming in Spectacle Lake, diving under the dock and underwater through the deepest crossties— although our swimsuits might catch on the wood and trap us there. I always watched for bubbles coming up when I sat on the dock.

Every person on our wagon must have been thinking of Paul Johanson when we passed the dirt side road. Paul had made a decision, followed messages with a code we did not understand: a language obscure and mysterious and wholly unrelated to the abbreviated desperate calls made to a pilot over the wild country of Mexico whose job it is to locate the rough landing field and touch the plane down.

I was thinking: Bill Troolin, there was a red-haired man and a little girl with braids on Seal Beach this morning, and I was also there. But how far Oxala, Mexico, is from central Minnesota; how far are both from this ocean. When you pass the dirt side road where a young man took his last swig of blackberry brandy—and you've just felt momentarily something like love—you feel the start of a shudder that lasts the rest of your life. There are always reasons, if you want them. There's always a code. And yet, if you go out every day on the hard gray sand you may see flames of light, bright as our loves, coming from the water as it moves steadily ashore. Even alone now, I can imagine a missionary flight to the Atlantic seacoast, a plane landing on the beach. As if no years have passed, and there's no need to run.